I sprinted across the room and then stopped dead

She was lying facedown on the floor. I dropped to one knee and turned her over.

It was then I saw the bullet hole.

I knew at once how it had happened. She had gone to the door and peered through the peephole for a look at the visitor. The gun, silenced and lethal, had been in position on the other side.

A split second later the bullet had smashed through her brain.

SEND ANOTHER HEARSE

Harold Q. Masur

A RAVEN HOUSE MYSTERY FROM

W🌐RLDWIDE

TORONTO · LONDON · NEW YORK

Raven House edition published November 1980

First printing June 1980
Second printing November 1980
Third printing April 1981
Fourth printing February 1982

ISBN 0-373-63000-X

Printed in Canada

1

SHE WAS VOGUE on the outside and vague on the inside.

She was fashionable and meticulously put together, very chic, very *soignée*, with deep auburn hair and wide hazel eyes that blinked at me with a bemused expression.

But despite her vague, uncertain manner, I knew instinctively that here was no standard-type, show-window mannequin, no painted posturer. Beneath the cosmetic mask I sensed an elfin quality, something alive and vibrant, all under strict discipline at the moment.

Another time I might have enjoyed meeting her. Not now, however. Not this morning. Not under these circumstances. Now I wanted only one thing. I wanted her to go away—quickly, quietly and without fuss.

As a matter of fact, I should never have opened the door in the first place. I should have let her ring until she burned out a generator at Consolidated Edison. But her finger on the bell, five minutes without respite, had been so persistent, so acoustically unbearable, that I finally answered, and there she was, regarding me with an odd little frown, almost as if she had forgotten the reason for her visit.

"Yes," I prompted.

"Er. . . doesn't Mr. Varney live here?"

How could I deny it? A nameplate on the door clearly pronounced his tenancy.

"He does," I said. "But he's not in at the moment."

"When do you expect him?"

"Sometime this evening."

"Oh." She peered at me uncertainly. "Are you a friend of his?"

"A relative," I lied again. What else could I say? She had found me in Varney's apartment and it was quite obvious that I had made myself at home.

She hesitated briefly, then said, "I'll phone him tomorrow," and turning crisply, she marched toward the elevator.

She carried herself with fluid grace and for a moment I admired the view. Then I closed the door and went back to work.

My search of Varney's apartment had only aggravated the general disorder. Soiled dishes were scattered haphazardly and there was a loaf of calcified bread next to a cup permanently bonded with the remains of a soft-boiled egg. In the bedroom I found too many clothes, and that is what disturbed me most of all.

Why would Dan Varney leave a perfectly good wardrobe behind him? It could mean a hasty departure. Or it could mean no departure at all. At least not of his own volition.

Everywhere the lack of a woman's touch was apparent. A film of dust had painted the furniture gray. Varney's wife, I'd been told, was in Reno getting a divorce. Obviously the lady had taste, for even in its present disreputable state the apartment expressed a certain style and warmth.

I returned to the desk and continued foraging. There was an accumulation of statements and bills, none of them receipted, and several impolite letters caustically dunning him for payment. Of the man himself, no trace. Not a single clue.

I was rummaging in the bottom drawer when a cool breeze touched the back of my neck and gave me an odd, prickling sensation. Suddenly I had that sharp and very special awareness of not being alone. A whispered footstep sounded on the carpet behind me and I whirled around.

The muzzle of a .38-caliber revolver, large, lethal and unfriendly, was pointed unerringly at the center button of my jacket.

"Sit still, mister. Don't make a move."

I was staring at a uniformed cop, large, husky, grim, determined. And just behind him stood my recent visitor, the auburn-haired mannequin, her eyes saucer-large and excited.

"That's the man!" Her voice was breathless. "He said he was a relative of Dan's, but he's lying. I never saw him before in my life. He's a burglar."

The cop spoke menacingly. "On your feet, mister. Take it slow and clasp your hands behind your neck."

The Smith & Wesson service revolver is a highly efficient piece of hardware and I had no intention of arguing with it. I could almost read his thoughts. This would be a good collar, fine for his career, worth a commendation at least, and maybe a promotion.

I really hated to disappoint him.

I said, "Just a minute now, Officer. You're making a mistake. I can explain all this—"

"Explain it to the sergeant."

"Now look, if you'll just—"

"Knock if off! Turn around and walk over to the wall. Put your hands against it and lean on them."

I obeyed. It was standard operating procedure, taught to every rookie at the Police Academy, designed to telegraph any sudden move, giving him the safest margin to fan a suspect for hidden weapons. He ran a hand under my arms, over my pockets, my thighs and legs, satisfying himself that I was unarmed.

"Where's the telephone?" he asked the girl.

"Over there on the desk."

I said, "Officer, you can save everybody a lot of trouble if you'll just listen to me."

"You live here, mister?"

"No, but—"

"You get permission to enter from the owner?"

"Not exactly, but—"

"How'd you get in?"

"With a key that—"

"The tenant give it to you?"

"Well, no, but—"

"That's all brother. Save your explanations for somebody else."

He played it safe and called the precinct. Why run the risk of hauling me in by himself when a couple of stalwarts in a prowl car would insure a trouble-free expedition? Leaning against the wall grew uncomfortable and I began to feel the strain in my arms. I shifted slightly and got a warning bark to freeze.

It took no time at all. The control room at Communications broadcast a squeal to a radio car cruising in the vicinity and in less than five minutes the bell rang and we had company. Two more city employees, veterans this time, who handled the situation with a brisk economy of words and action. They hustled me down, bundled me unceremoniously into a car and roared off with only an occasional wail of the siren.

A word of advice to the average citizen. Should you be unlucky enough to get arrested, follow this simple formula. Refuse to say anything that may be used against you, sign no documents and insist upon the aid and advice of a lawyer.

This last is paramount.

Not only because lawyers have to make a living. Which of course they do. But lawyers know the angles, the complexities, the hurdles. They are versed in constitutional guarantees and how to protect a man's rights under the law.

A man in trouble with the law needs a lawyer with the same urgency that a man with an inflamed appendix needs a doctor.

I followed none of the rules. I was in trouble, but I did not call a lawyer. After all, I had my own diploma from law school and a certificate of admission to the Bar from the Appellate Division of the State of New York. I had been in practice for ten years and if I didn't know the ropes by now I might as well take down my shingle. I felt competent to handle this scrape myself.

There is an old adage: The lawyer who defends himself has a fool for a client.

Well...maybe....

THEY TOOK ME to the interrogation room, where two inquisitors from the detective squad took over. They were named de Castro and Hahn. De Castro was a tall, rangy specimen with a bony face and ravenous eyes. Hahn was heavy, shambling and deceptively benevolent. He had a habit of leaning on an elbow and fingering his left earlobe while he talked.

"Well, well..." he said wonderingly, after examining my identification papers. "Scott Jordan! I'll be damned! You're the lawyer who was involved in that Hammond case last year."

"The same," I said. "And before we go on, I believe I'm entitled to make one telephone call."

"Sure. After you're booked."

"Booked for what?"

"Breaking and entering."

"Now wait a minute. You want me to cooperate, stretch the rule a little. No answers from me until I make one call."

"Don't tell us you want a lawyer."

"Not yet. I'd like to phone my office."

He shoved the instrument in my direction. "All right, go ahead."

I dialed a familiar number and got through to Cassidy. Cassidy is fat, forty and worth her weight in Harvard law clerks. She answered on the second ring.

"This is your boss," I told her. "Everything under control?"

"So far. Adam Coleman phoned about five minutes ago."

"Just the man I want. Call him back and tell him to get over to the Seventeenth Precinct on Fifty-first Street right away. On the double. It's an emergency.''

"Somebody in trouble?"

"Me. I've been arrested. Tell you about it later." I hung up.

"Now," Hahn said. "Everything squared away, Counselor? Good. Let's get down to facts. You were found in the apartment of a man named Dan Varney, apparently sacking the joint.''

"No, sir."

"What do you mean, no, sir. You were caught with the meat in your hands.''

"Was I? You searched me, Hahn. Did you find any evidence of larceny?''

"We found a letter in your pocket addressed to Varney."

"It had been shoved under the door. I picked it up with the intention of leaving it on his desk.''

"And absentmindedly dropped it in your pocket, I suppose.''

"That's right."

He smiled with tolerant skepticism. "You said you got into the apartment with a key. Is this it?''

"Yes, sir."

"Where'd you get it?"

"From Varney's partner, Adam Coleman.''

"But Varney did not give you permission to use it.''

"How could he? He's been missing for weeks. That's why I went to his apartment. I was looking for a clue to his whereabouts.'

De Castro spoke up, the hungry eyes slitted. "You picked a good time for it, Counselor. Daytime, nobody home, no possession of a dangerous weapon. That limits the charge to burglary in the third degree."

"He studies the penal law," Hahn explained.

"He doesn't study it hard enough," I said. "An essential ingredient of burglary is missing."

"That so?"

"Yes, sir. Intent to commit a crime. Paragraph four-oh-four. I did not go there to steal."

"Don't forget the letter we found in your pocket, Jordan. That puts it in a different category. Tampering with the U.S. mail."

Letting them find that envelope in my possession was a mistake. I should have gotten rid of it, but things had happened too fast and it never occurred to me.

I looked at him mildly. "There was an address on the back flap. I merely wanted to copy it and question the sender. I thought she might know where Varney is hiding."

"Hiding?" Hahn raised an eyebrow. "What makes you think he's hiding? Maybe he took a trip somewhere."

"He took a trip all right," I said. "And he took something else too. Two hundred thousand dollars that didn't belong to him."

Silence. Both men suddenly alert, eyeing me sharply. A shaft of sunlight on which dust motes floated weightlessly slanted through the window. The squad room had a musty odor. Ironic, I thought. Me, Scott Jordan, attorney-at-law, on the griddle, here in this room with its memories of thieves, muggers, hustlers, dope peddlers, and all the sharpshooters who felt the world owed them a living.

Hahn's chin was up. "Repeat that, please."

"Certainly. Dan Varney disappeared with two hundred thousand dollars that didn't belong to him, money stolen from a client."

"You represent this client?"

"No, sir. I represent Varney's partner."

"His name?"

"Adam Coleman."

"Partner in what kind of business?"

"Literary agency. Coleman and Varney."

"Two hundred thousand dollars." Hahn pursed his lips. "How come we have no record of it?"

"Because it hasn't been reported."

"Not to the D.A. either?"

"No, sir."

"Then suppose you report it right now, Counselor, and—" The phone rang and he reached for it. "Detective Hahn.... Yeah, he's here. What about it?" He listened and looked over at me. "It's your secretary. She says she can't find Coleman."

I bounced a hand off my temple. "I forgot. Tell her he's in the visiting room at St. John's Hospital. She can reach him there."

But Hahn did not relay the message. Instead, he told Cassidy it would be attended to and issued orders to have a radio car pick up Adam Coleman and bring him in at once. Then he leaned back and said, "We're listening, Counselor."

So I told him, starting with Adam bursting into my office early that morning....

2

ADAM WAS WAVING a paper in the air. "Look at this," he said a little wildly. "I've been served with a summons. I'm being sued. Two hundred thousand dollars." He repeated the sum. "Two hundred thousand and I never even saw the money." He was breathing like a fire horse.

"Sit down, Adam," I told him. "Relax."

"Relax! That's easy for you to say. You lawyers thrive on litigation. Every time somebody's in trouble it. . . ." He swallowed apologetically. "I'm sorry, Scott." He tossed the papers on my desk. "What am I going to do about this?"

"I don't know. Let me read the complaint first. Pull up a chair, Adam, please."

But he preferred to stand and pace while I read, skimming the legal terminology to extract the essence. It was simple enough. The plaintiff was a man named Fred Duncan. He was suing Adam Coleman and Dan Varney, both as individuals and as members of a firm, for two hundred thousand dollars received by them for the sale of his book, *The Kingpins*, to Zenith Films, a Hollywood producing outfit.

Coleman & Varney, Literary Agents. Not a large nor an especially outstanding firm. I had known Adam for some years, had performed a few legal chores for him in the past. One of them being the partnership agreement between the two men when they started the agency.

I had met Varney on that occasion and I remembered him as a large man, engaging, forceful, energetic, with an easy smile, a glib and articulate tongue and ruggedly carved features. He had quit his career as a moderately successful writer to enter the agency business, where he hoped to capitalize on a drinking acquaintance with a number of editors.

Adam, ordinarily mild and clerical-looking behind shell-rimmed glasses, had other qualities. An orderly brain, for one thing, and a sharp eye for literary properties. A talent for nursing temperamental authors, and an instinct for applying the proper amalgam of sympathy and coercion.

His agitation had eased a little now. He stood over my desk, shoulders sagging, face perpendicular with gloom. The summons explained his mood and now I wanted him to explain the summons.

"This Fred Duncan, I assume he's a client of yours."

"Yes."

"And he wrote a book called *The Kingpins*."

"Yes."

"Which you sold to Zenith Films."

"From manuscript. We haven't been able to find a trade publisher."

"How come?"

"Duncan's a neophyte, a rank amateur. The writing is lousy. But what a story he tells! Based on fact, too. It's a blockbuster, Scott. That's what Zenith bought, and with a good scenario they can't miss."

"Couldn't you get a pro to rewrite and polish?"

"We're still dickering."

"But it's all wrapped up with Zenith? Contracts signed and the money paid."

"I—I guess so."

"What do you mean, you guess. Don't you know?"

He nodded unhappily. "I was out of town when the check arrived. Varney deposited it in our special account at the Merchant's Trust and when it cleared he simply withdrew the cash and . . . disappeared."

"You mean absconded?"

Adam groaned from the heart. "There's no other explanation. I can't find him, he hasn't shown up at the office, he doesn't answer his phone, nobody's seen him, and the money is gone."

"Varney's married, isn't he?"

"To my sister. Barbara. Didn't you know?"

I shook my head. "When did that happen?"

"About a year ago. She'd just returned from Europe and met me at the office one day. I introduced them. Barbara's a stunner. One look and Varney zeroed in. Don't you read the newspapers?"

"Only international news and comics, not wedding announcements. As a matter of fact, I never met Barbara. Doesn't she know where he is?"

He gestured helplessly. "Barbara's in Reno getting a divorce. That marriage was on the rocks from the beginning. God knows, she tried to make it work, but . . . well, anyway the money's gone and so is Dan. And now I've got Fred Duncan on my neck."

"Tell me about him."

Adam took off his glasses and wiped them.

"Duncan is an ex-cop. A Scotsman with an accent

thick enough to sit on. He was wounded during a holdup some years ago, shot in the knee and partially crippled. They pensioned him off the force and he got a job at the Merchant's Trust, custodian in the safe-deposit vault. That's where I met him. He knew I was a literary agent, and one day he handed me a manuscript and asked me to read it. He'd been working on it for a long time, he said. I wasn't sanguine over the prospect. Everybody wants to write a book, it seems, and I've read some dillies.

"Anyway, I took it back to the office and left it on my desk. Varney found it and started reading. He got interested and thought it had possibilities. So we started sending it around. Well, that sort of thing takes time, and Duncan was a nuisance. He never stopped pestering us. He'd phone almost every day, grumbling and griping, until I got so fed up I wanted to chuck the whole thing. But then Dan had a bright idea and he sent the story over to Zenith Films. It's an independent outfit with a lot of imagination."

He paused and I nodded to show that he had my full attention.

"The first nibble came with a request for information about the author. And when they learned his background and realized how much of the story was authentic biography, they began to negotiate in earnest. We settled on two hundred thousand and notified Duncan. He had to sign the contract, of course. Then I flew out to the coast and only got back last week. Varney wasn't around. At first I had no reason to be suspicious—he'd often take off for a day or two. And then Duncan started calling, wanting to know about his money. That's when I began to have misgivings. I got in touch with Zenith Films and they told me the check had been mailed. So I went over to the bank and got the shock of my life. The check had been deposited and the money withdrawn.''

"So they gave Varney two hundred thousand in cash?"

"Yes. He handed them some cock-and-bull story about a nutty client who didn't believe in banks."

"Varney's checks didn't have to be countersigned?"

"No. Either one of us has authority to withdraw money."

"Isn't that a little risky?"

"On hindsight, yes. But someone has to sign checks when the other is out of town. Besides, who expected anything like this? My God, you don't go into business with a man suspecting he's a crook. You have to trust him."

"You told Duncan about the money?"

"I had no alternative. I stalled him as long as I could and then . . . well, you can imagine. I thought he'd have a seizure, apoplexy or something."

"And this morning you were served with a summons."

"Yes."

I turned it over and glanced at the name of Duncan's lawyer. Irving Birnbaum, with an office on Lower Broadway. It seemed vaguely familiar.

Adam said querulously, "They can't hold me responsible, can they?"

"Oh, yes they can. For every last penny."

"But why?" His voice rose a full octave. "Varney stole the money, not me."

"That doesn't make one particle of difference," I said. "Each partner is personally responsible for the

acts and omissions of his associates. Varney can be
made to share the burden, if you find him. If not, the
law insists that you shoulder the whole load yourself.''

Adam looked stupefied. For a moment I thought I
had lost him. He shook his head in a dazed way and as
my words penetrated they wrung a groan of anguish
from his throat.

"How can I find him?'' he said. ''I'm no detective.''

''You'll have to hire one.''

"That's expensive and may take months.''

"True. I'll make a suggestion.''

He looked at me hopefully. ''Yes?''

"We can notify the District Attorney. After all,
Varney's a thief. The authorities have money and
manpower. Finding Varney is really their job anyway.''

"No.'' Adam was surprisingly emphatic. ''I—I'd
rather not involve the police.''

''Why not?''

He hesitated, choosing his words carefully. ''We
can't stand the publicity. How do you think our
other clients would react if they thought their
money wasn't safe? They'd all pull out. It would
wreck the firm.''

"I see what you mean. Then we'll have to find
Varney ourselves.''

''And if we can't?''

''Then you're in trouble, Adam.''

He chopped the air with his hand. ''But I haven't
got two hundred thousand dollars—or anything like
it.''

''Not now, perhaps. But you may have some day.

And the minute you do, Duncan will levy execution on his judgment.''

His eyes brightened foxily. "I'll go into bankruptcy.''

"And wreck your credit rating for the future?''

He thought about it. "All right. What do you suggest?''

"I suggest we file an answer to the summons. We'll enter a general denial, delay the proceedings and in the meantime try to locate Varney. Have you any idea what made him do this?''

"Sure. Debts, high living, expensive habits. Dan was a compulsive spender. He always needed money. He was in debt to half a dozen loan sharks and half a year behind in alimony payments to his first wife. Her lawyers were beginning to apply pressure and making threats. I guess the load just got too much, so he decided to grab a stake and bail out.''

"Any idea where he might have gone?''

"Not a glimmer.''

"Would your sister have any ideas?''

"Barbara? I doubt it. They weren't even talking to each other when she left.''

"Have you searched his desk?''

"At the office, yes. Nothing there.''

"How about his apartment?'' Adam brightened momentarily. "No, but I have a key. Dan let me sleep there a couple of weeks ago while my own place was being painted.''

"I suggest you go over there and shake it down. Look for cards or folders from a travel agency, receipts from an airline, the name of a shipping company, anything.'' —

It was a project that gave Adam no pleasure. He stood still, looking glum and pitiably harassed.

"What's the trouble?" I asked.

"I can't go," he said. "Not now. I haven't got the time."

"What's more important?"

"The hospital. I have to go to the hospital."

I looked at him sharply. "Are you sick?"

"Not me." His hands were clenched at his sides. "It's my father. He had another heart attack."

"Serious?"

"He's on the critical list." Adam's mouth twisted bitterly. "And that woman he married never even let me know. I had to get the news indirectly."

"You haven't seen him for some time, have you, Adam?"

"I can't see him now, either. He's in a coma, under oxygen. They won't let anybody into his room." He looked up, tight-lipped. "But I want to be there anyway. What the hell! I'm still his son, even if he did disown me. Look, Scott, I'll give you the key. You know better than I what to look for, and I'd consider it a great favor."

How could I refuse? Too much time had been wasted already. So I took the key and made a note of Varney's address.

"You'll need a private detective," I said.

"I'm in your hands, Scott. You make the arrangements."

I told Cassidy my destination and accompanied Adam to the street. We separated. He took a cab to St. John's Hospital and I cut east toward Varney's apartment.

3

DETECTIVE HAHN LEANED OVER and held a whispered conference with de Castro. The latter nodded and left the room. Hahn lit a cigarette, eyes squinting at me through upward-curling smoke.

"Not very bright, Counselor—entering a strange apartment like that."

"Only because that girl came along at a highly inopportune moment. Who is she?"

"Mrs. Dan Varney."

"The ex-Mrs. Varney, you mean."

"That's right."

"Number one or two?"

"Two probably. This one just back from Reno. Claims she went to the apartment to pick up some clothes."

Adam's sister. Barbara. No wonder she'd been suspicious. Finding me there in the apartment, a total stranger, a man she'd never seen, acting as if I owned the place, claiming to be a relative of Varney's. I smiled to myself.

"I know what you're thinking," Hahn said. "That she won't press charges. Forget it, Counselor. She no longer has any rights in the matter."

"Maybe not. But Adam Coleman got that key in a lawful manner and he had every right to enter the apartment. I was merely acting as his agent. Why dawdle with me? If you boys really want to earn your salary, start searching for Dan Varney. There's your real criminal. Against him you'd have no trouble proving a case. The D.A. could—''

I stopped because the door had opened. De Castro was ushering Barbara into the room. I gathered that the situation had been explained. She advanced toward me with her gloved hand extended, apologetic and slightly embarrassed.

"So you're Scott Jordan. Adam has mentioned your name several times. I'm dreadfully sorry about all this. My behavior was impulsive and perhaps a little foolish."

"Not at all foolish," I said. "Under the circumstances, you couldn't help being suspicious."

"Am I forgiven?"

"Of course."

Suddenly she smiled. It warmed and animated her face, softening the sculptured lines. The vague and bemused look was gone. She turned to Hahn with composure and assurance.

"Naturally I won't sign a complaint against Mr. Jordan. It was all a mistake. Can he leave now?"

"Not yet," Hahn said dryly. "We want to check his story about the key first."

Barbara looked at me again. "I tried to reach Dan on the phone. Someone picked up the receiver but wouldn't answer."

"That was me," I said.

"And I thought it was Dan being obstinate. That's why I came over and kept ringing the bell. I understand he's missing. Is it really true?"

"Yes."

"But why?"

She listened in shocked disbelief while I explained. "I suspected a lot of things about Dan," she said, "but not that he was a thief." She shook her head. "And to make Adam responsible...."

As if mentioning his name had served as a cue, the door opened and there stood Adam in the custody of a uniformed policeman. From his worried and perplexed expression, I knew that he was all at sea. He had no idea why he'd been plucked out of the hospital and hauled down to a police station. His eyes, circling the room, brightened a little when he saw me and then widened in astonishment as Barbara ran forward. He let her kiss him and then held her out at arm's length.

"Barbara! When did you get back?"

"Last night, too late to call. And when I tried your office this morning, nobody answered."

He looked around, bewildered. "Will somebody please tell me what the devil this is all about? Why my sister is here? Why I'm here? And my lawyer? What happened?"

"Sit down, Mr. Coleman," Hahn said. "We want some information about your partner, Dan Varney. We're told the man is missing."

"There's been some trouble," I volunteered. "Would you kindly tell these gentlemen how—"

"Quiet!" De Castro stopped me with a hard stare. "Another chirp out of you, Counselor, and you'll wait outside."

I subsided. Hahn waited until he had Adam's attention. Then he said, "How long has Varney been gone?"

"Something over a week. I don't know the precise date. I was out of town."

"Why weren't the police notified?"

"I assumed he was visiting some author."

"And you kept that assumption even after you knew that two hundred thousand dollars had left with him?"

Adam darted me a hurt look, as if I had betrayed him.

Hahn said, "A man can disappear any time he likes, Mr. Coleman. We have no control over the movements of any citizen. Not unless he commits a crime. Larceny, for example. Stealing your client's money."

"We have other clients," Adam said lamely. "Knowledge of Varney's dishonesty would have thrown them into a panic. Our agency is small and we can hardly afford. . . ." He let it hang, gesturing vaguely.

"You have a key to Varney's apartment. May I see it?" Hahn's palm was out, waiting.

"I'm sorry, I gave—" Adam caught himself and threw me a questioning glance.

"Go ahead," I said. "Tell him the truth."

"I gave the key to Mr. Jordan. I asked him to search Varney's apartment for a clue as to his whereabouts." Adam's jaw clamped stubbornly. He stood abruptly, pushing his chair back.

"Dammit! What happened? What gives here? I have a right to know."

The flood of words came from Barbara. She could hold back no longer and neither detective tried to plug the dike. Comprehension dawned on Adam's face and he looked at me with a wry grin.

"So she thought you were a burglar and they pulled you in. My God, that's rich!" He turned to Hahn. "I'm afraid you boys made a mistake."

"The mistake was Jordan's. If Varney turns up and files a complaint, we'll have to book Jordan for illegal entry."

"If Varney turns up," I said, "he'll be too busy defending himself on a charge of grand larceny to file a complaint against anyone."

Hahn smiled grudgingly. "All right, Counselor. I suggest you notify the Complaint Bureau at the D.A.'s office. If Varney left the state we may need extradition papers."

I offered him my hand. He gave it a single insincere pump. De Castro was at the back of the squad room, gazing through the steel-meshed window. He was not a handshaker. I beckoned and Adam followed me out, holding Barbara's arm.

I said, "Thanks for the vote of confidence, Mrs. Varney."

"The name is Barbara. Barbara Coleman. I'm dropping the Varney completely."

"An excellent idea," Adam said. "Welcome back to the clan." He stepped back to study her appraisingly. "That's a might fancy outfit for this time of day. Hattie Carnegie? Balenciaga?"

"These are working clothes," Barbara said. "They were shooting pictures for *Harper's Bazaar* this morning."

"I guess you didn't know," Adam explained to me. "Barbara's a top-flight fashion model."

She certainly has the equipment for it, I thought.

"Your friend is staring," she told her brother.

"Why not? He's young and vigorous and I doubt if there's any better scenery within a radius of a hundred miles."

"A thousand," I said gallantly.

She dropped her eyes demurely. "Will you take the man's advice?" she asked. "You know, about going down to the D.A.'s office."

"Not now," Adam said. "I want to get back to the hospital and—" He stopped, suddenly sober. "You haven't heard about dad."

"What happened?"

"Another heart attack."

She paled visibly under the makeup. "Is it . . . is it . . . ?"

He nodded, speaking frankly. "Yes, Barbara, it's serious. They've got him under oxygen. At dad's age, anything can happen." No soft soap, no punches pulled.

"Where?"

"St. John's."

I caught a flash of distress and then she was gone, racing down the precinct stairs. Adam and I followed. The desk sergeant looked up, startled. For a moment he thought Barbara was trying to escape from custody. She was headed for the door, heels clicking in high gear, when she spotted two people sitting on a bench. She applied her brakes and the newcomers rose to meet her.

Barbara kissed the woman and shook hands with the man. They looked vaguely familiar, and then I remembered. Gilbert and Victoria Dodd. I had met them casually at one of Adam's cocktail parties. Victoria was Adam's older sister. Gil Dodd her husband. Questions flew, with everybody jabbering at once.

The Dodds, I gathered, had been at the hospital with Adam. When the two cops had appeared and carted him away, they were naturally perturbed and had followed along to the precinct. Adam eased their fears with a quick explanation and then indicated me.

"You remember Scott Jordan. My sister and brother-in-law."

Victoria smiled toothily. She was a tall, horsey woman with harlequin glasses over slightly protuberant eyes. She had about ten years on Adam, but her hair was jet black, worn in a tight knot at the back of her neck. Her figure was long and straight, without embellishments, nothing more than a serviceable package for the necessary plumbing. Nature, as if suffering from a guilty conscience for shortchanging one member of the family, had compensated by its generosity to Barbara.

"Of course," Gil Dodd said. "Scott Jordan. You're Adam's lawyer."

He smiled, proud of his square white teeth. He was in his middle forties, medium height, solid and compact, with a brown face and receding hairline that increased the dimensions of his forehead. It gave him a brainy, intelligent appearance. He was well preserved, well dressed, with fastidious haberdashery and a freshly barbered look.

He relinquished my hand and raised his own to squeeze Adam's shoulder. "Well, old boy, I'm glad it's nothing serious. The way they grabbed you at the hospital, we thought you were involved in nothing less than a mass murder. Scared the life out of Vickie.''

She exhaled to show her relief.

"Look," Barbara said impatiently, "can't we discuss all this later. I want to see dad.''

"You can't," Vickie told her. "The nurse has strict orders.''

"From whom? Lorraine?''

She said the name with a kind of acid contempt, with a biting malice that surprised me.

"And the doctor," Gil Dodd said.

"Is Lorraine with him now?''

"She's with him all the time. Nobody else can get near him.''

Barbara's mouth tightened. "We'll see about that." She started resolutely for the door. The rest of the pack shook their heads and went after her.

I caught hold of Adam's arm in the street. "Hold it a minute. Do you know a girl named Kate Wallace?''

He looked at me oddly. "What about her?''

"There was a letter under Varney's door with her name and a return address in Brooklyn on the envelope.''

He nodded solemnly. "It's no secret. Kate Wallace was one of the reasons Barbara left Dan. She was Varney's girl friend.''

"Close?''

"Very.''

"Then I guess I'll have a chat with her.''

Gil Dodd had flagged a cab and got the girls installed. He was holding the door open and whistling for Adam.

"I'll call you later," Adam said and hurried to join his relatives.

I watched the cab pull away. The family had been estranged from their father for some time now, disowned when he'd married a younger woman. But loss of their inheritance had evidently not canceled a deep-rooted filial devotion.

4

BROOKLYN IS A LARGE BOROUGH inhabited by many citizens with a variety of dialects. It can be reached by boat, bridge, tunnel or helicopter. It has a fine botanical garden, an excellent library, several colleges, a zoo and some fine residential areas.

Brooklyn Heights is one of them. Just across the bay from Manhattan, it commands a spectacular view of New York Harbor with its vaulting skyline. And between the buildings a pedestrian can see the Statue of Liberty thrusting her torch skyward.

I found Kate Wallace's building, a medium-size structure, once elaborately elegant, now merely respectable. I was eager for a look at the girl, curious to see what attractions would lead a man to stray from the fireside with homework like Barbara around. But this was not my day. I rang for two full minutes and then gave up. Nobody home.

So I vacated the premises and took a subway back to the office.

Cassidy was at her desk. She caught my beckoning nod and followed me with a stenographic pad and several newly sharpened pencils. She sat in the red leather client's chair and watched me reach for the phone. I dialed a number and waited for the laconic voice. It came on the first ring.

"Hello, Max," I said. "Can you stop by here?"

"When?"

"Soon as possible. I have a job for you."

"Twenty minutes." Max Turner disgorged words with all the prodigal abandon of a slot machine.

I hung up. Cassidy had a pencil poised over her pad, ready for hieroglyphics. I gave her the title of the action: *Fred Duncan* v *Adam Coleman*. And then I started dictating an answer to the summons and complaint that had been served on Adam.

I entered a general denial, knowing that we really didn't have a leg to stand on. Adam owed the money and eventually, unless we found Varney, he would have to pay it. It was a frivolous defense, without merit. And if Duncan's lawyer was on his toes, he would probably make a motion to strike the answer and award his client summary judgment.

Cassidy got it all on the first take. Her shorthand was precise and accurate. "All right," I told her. "Type it up. The original goes to court and a copy to opposing counsel."

She sighed with the air of a martyr. Cassidy possessed a unique temperament, compounded oddly enough from equal parts of dour cynicism and unflagging romanticism. Right now the cynicism prevailed.

"Just once," she said, "I would like to see the cards stacked in our favor. A client with a clear-cut case. How come we always get the impossible ones?"

"Not always," I said. "And besides, when did we lose a case?"

"When? Two weeks ago. My God, you have a short memory."

I grimaced painfully and gave her an aggrieved look. It was not a pleasant reminder. But Cassidy could afford to take liberties. She was practically a member of the firm. I had inherited her from my first and only employer, Oliver Wendell Rogers, when the old boy retired after forty years in practice, leaving me in charge, with the privilege of hanging out my own shingle.

I could easily have found someone more decorative. But never as efficient or loyal. She was that rare commodity, a secretary with experience, wisdom, and initiative. And she knew that reminding me of an occasional setback was probably good for my immortal soul.

She took the notes out to her own typewriter and reappeared almost instantly. "Max is here."

"Send him in."

Max Turner was a private detective who had performed sundry chores for me in the past. He was an angular man, unassuming and self-effacing. His face had no distinguishing characteristics outside of a fairly prominent nose. His manner was habitually noncommittal. Below the surface, however, there was a hard, practical core. He had tenacity, intelligence and a filing-card memory. And the ability to get at the crux of a problem without a long, time-consuming explanation.

He listened to me with his eyes half-closed and opened them when I finished. "So we have to find Dan Varney."

"Yes. I suggest you canvass airlines, railroads, bus depots. . . . You know the procedure."

He knew it, and he also knew the difficulties involved. Possibly hundreds of thousands of people entering and leaving New York every twenty-four hours, a nameless, faceless horde, vast and hardly identifiable to clerks or ticket sellers.

"Are we looking for a live body?" Max asked.

"Let's proceed on that assumption," I said. "He probably left the same day he cashed the check, which should narrow it down somewhat."

Max nodded. "Any romantic entanglements?"

"Only one, apparently. A girl named Kate Wallace. I'll tackle her myself."

"Naturally."

I ignored it. "And, Max, put a couple of men on it, if necessary."

"Good men are expensive."

"Do you need any money?"

"An itemized bill will arrive in due course."

"Keep it down as much as possible. Our client is not a rich man."

Max tapped his forehead, recallingly. "Adam Coleman. Sounds familiar. Any relation to M. Parker Coleman, the hotel tycoon?"

"His son."

Max raised an eyebrow. "What do you mean, he isn't rich."

"The father is rich," I said. "Not the son."

"So? But I hear the old man isn't long for this world."

"Who told you?"

"Read it in one of the gossip columns."

I nodded. The old man had been a wheel and his name was still newsworthy. It would always be linked with the business he'd founded. The Coleman Hotels. A nice operation, nothing spectacular like the Hilton chain, but solid enough and agreeably profitable.

M. Parker Coleman had been a client of Oliver Wendell Rogers. So naturally, working in the office, I knew something about his affairs. That, however, did not influence the old man one bit when Rogers had retired. He did not keep me on as counsel for the hotels, except for scraps and minor matters like answering a summons for icy sidewalks. The plums went to a large Wall Street firm with nine partners and two floors in a brand-new skyscraper.

The plums wouldn't have lasted anyway. Old M.P. was no longer active. The combination of a new wife and an old cardiac flutter had dissipated his energies and curbed his enterprise. A fresh management team had taken over, leaving the old boy enough leisure to indulge his spouse and count his dividends.

Max said, "Your client will be rich if Papa Coleman dies."

"Afraid not," I told him. "Adam objected to the second marriage. He did not appreciate the lady's qualities. He went even further. He insulted the bride outrageously."

"Not very tactful."

"To say the least. It got him tossed out of the ancestral homestead on his ear."

"And the other children?"

"Two daughters. Both of them jumped to Adam's defense and got the same medicine."

"Disinherited?"

"Without a button, I'm told."

"Tough." Max stretched and got to his feet and

shambled to the door. "I'll keep in touch, Counselor," he said and left.

There was some comfort in knowing that Max was on the case. If persistence and resourcefulness could dig up any information, we'd have a line on Dan Varney in due time.

Alone, I checked the telephone directory, got the number of St. John's Hospital and dialed. I told the switchboard girl I wanted to inquire about the condition of Mr. M. Parker Coleman. As expected, she connected me with the floor nurse. I apologized, informed her that it was urgent, and asked her to please page Adam Coleman. "I believe he's in the waiting room," I said.

"Yes, he is. I'm very sorry, sir. But we can't tie up this line."

"I understand. However, this is an emergency. Would you ask him to use a booth and call his lawyer?"

She agreed and broke the connection. Three minutes later my phone rang and it was Adam. "Scott?" he said hopefully. "Something to report? Have you found Dan?"

"I'm not a magician," I said. "I merely called you there to save time. About this girl, Kate Wallace, any idea where she works?"

"Hold on. I'll ask Barbara."

Silence for a space while static crackled over the wires, and then he was back. "Are you listening, Scott?"

"Shoot."

"Kate Wallace works for an advertising agency. Mitchell, Bodner and Olds."

"I know the outfit. Incidentally, where is Barbara staying?"

"At the Madison."

"I'd like to ask her some questions about Varney. Find out if she'll be free later."

I heard the squeak of hinges on the booth door and then the muffled sound of voices.

"Scott?" It was Barbara this time.

"Yes."

"How about cocktails at five-thirty?"

"Fine."

"See you then."

The prospect added flavor to the day.

5

MITCHELL, BODNER AND OLDS had leased a floor in one of those hammered-aluminum buildings along Madison Avenue. This was the communications belt, where copywriters toiled, extolling the products of American enterprise, stimulating consumer desire, whetting the acquisitive instinct, intoxicating the eye with pictures and multiplying installment credit.

Ad Alley.

Ulcer Gulch.

Mitchell, Bodner and Olds. Ascending in the elevator I tried to recall what I knew of the firm. The name itself was a vestigial remainder. Mitchell was dead, Bodner had retired, and Olds, although sticking around as chairman of the board, had relinquished control to younger hands. While not one of the advertising giants, it still billed a substantial fifty million a year. Cigarettes, toothpaste, department stores, deodorants.

The elevator discharged me on the twenty-second floor into a walnut-paneled reception room that fairly trumpeted prosperity. A very trim item of female confection sat behind the desk wearing a perpetual smile.

"May I help you, sir?"

"I'd like to see Miss Wallace."

"About which account, sir?"

"Tell her the Varney account."

She looked faintly puzzled. "I don't seem to recall. . . . I think you'd better talk to Mr. Alex Olds."

"No, ma'am," I said. "Kate Wallace."

"But she doesn't work here any more. She left several days ago. I'm sure Mr. Olds can—"

"All right," I interrupted. "Mr. Olds will do fine."

She got busy on the intercom and arranged it. Soon a girl emerged from the inner recesses and offered to show me the way. I followed her along a corridor with closely spaced doors on either side, some mute, some chattering with typewriters.

The drones behind them had an important job.

They had to keep the wheels of industry rolling. They had to make the great, gullible American public want stuff it didn't need. Keep the iron rolling out of Detroit. A good automobile year stimulates the entire economy. Planned obsolescence. One-year-old models superseded by mass-produced, chrome-plated, rocket-inspired, road-choking monstrosities. The tattooed male is a sure sign of masculinity; smoke the same brand. The rhapsodically beautiful girl swills beer; drink the same brew. Every plumber can smell like a rose. Every housewife can prepare a gastronomic delight from a can of peas and a package of frozen lead. Thrift is out of fashion. Buy, buy, buy. . . .

At the end of the corridor my guide opened a door and ushered me into a sizable room. Behind the desk a man was busy at the telephone. Mr. Alex Olds, son of one of the founders, was par for the advertising course. A perennially youngish party, with the standard longish hair and three-piece suit. But there was nothing standard in his bright, quick-moving eyes and the restless energy that kept him shifting about in his chair while he talked.

". . . Well, of course," he said. "We wanted the campaign to be an absolute triumph. We spent three days finding the right model and the proper accessories and what happened? The presses gave her a double mouth. Two sets of lips and neither one the right color. I tell you, I was demolished. . . . Oh, yes, I raised hell and the magazine promised us a rerun at no expense." He listened a moment, hung up and heaved a colossal sigh.

His fingers plucked fruitlessly at his pockets. "Have you got a cigarette?"

I gave him one and snapped my lighter.

He inhaled hungrily and kept the smoke in his lungs. "God, if our client caught me smoking this brand he'd cut out my heart and throw it away." He released some of the smoke. "What's this about a Varney account?"

"Just a ruse to get in," I said. "I'm trying to find out what happened to Kate Wallace."

He shook his head sadly. "There was a girl, that Kate Wallace. Great copy chief. One of the best. Imaginative, original, full of ideas. Had a big future here, I don't mind saying, and I hated like the devil to lose her. When she walked in out of a clear blue sky and told me she was quitting I almost collapsed. I figured the competition was raiding our talent. I offered her more money, a lot more. Couldn't even tempt her. Said she was tired. Said she wanted to get away. I offered her a vacation—with pay, two weeks, three weeks. No soap. I offered her a leave

of absence, told her to write her own ticket...."
He threw his hands up in a gesture of total despair.

"And?" I prompted.

"Nothing. She promised to think it over. But first
she wanted to get out of town."

"Where?"

"I tried to worm it out of her, hoping to keep in
touch. But she wouldn't say. She seemed secretive
and she had this crazy compulsion to leave at once.
Sure took me by surprise, even though I noticed
she'd been nervous lately, always on edge. But
that's more or less standard in this business. We're
always under a strain. Kate especially. She took a
real beating as copy chief. Caught the full impact
from our clients. They foot the bill, they think
they're advertising geniuses. Always coming up
with some half-baked idea they're sure will move
merchandise. You get a deodorant manufacturer to
sponsor a television show and right away he's a producer, a story editor, a director, a set designer and a
casting expert."

Alexander Olds stroked his closed eyelids.

"Headaches, ulcers and insomnia. What a racket!
You think brilliance is important? Original ideas?
You're off-base, friend. Soft-soaping the client is
more important. Keeping some lardy buffoon happy
is more important. That's my job. And it was Kate's
job, too. God, I'm gonna miss that girl. She had the
gift, believe me, and genuine talent is a dwindling
commodity in this business."

He glanced at my card again. "Lawyer, eh? What
did you want to see her about, Mr. Jordan?"

"A confidential matter," I said. "Could you tell
me this—does she have any family?"

"Yes. Her parents live in Ormont, Upstate New York." The phone rang and he snatched it like an anteater. "Olds speaking." His face changed and his eyes went to the ceiling and his voice purred. "Yes, of course, Mr. Frankel. I see your point. You don't like the layout; we'll develop another angle. I'll have the art department stick with it all night if necessary and you can have another presentation tomorrow morning. Absolutely. Not later than ten o'clock. Goodbye, Mr. Frankel."

He hung up and appealed to me. "See what I mean? Let me tell you something, Mr. Jordan—"

But I was already on my feet, palm up and facing him. "You've given me too much of your valuable time already, Mr. Olds. Thanks a million. No, don't bother. I can find the way."

He had his problems and I had mine. The man exhausted me. I guess there is no easy way to make money except to inherit it. Which reminded me, for some reason, of Barbara Coleman.

I glanced at my watch and saw that it was almost five-thirty.

6

"THERE'S BEEN A CHANGE in plans," Barbara told me on the house phone. "Come on up."

Her room at the Madison was in a state of disorder. A huge wardrobe trunk gaped open, fully packed. On the bed, two large suitcases bulged with feminine attire. Various other articles were scattered about. She brushed a wisp of auburn hair from her forehead and smiled.

"This won't take long. I'm almost finished."

"Moving?" I asked.

"Yes. Back to the apartment. So long as it's available there's no point in staying here. I hate hotels. Both Dan and I signed the lease. Besides, it's a rent-controlled building. I'd never be able to duplicate— why are you staring?"

"You look different," I said.

She did indeed. The highly fashioned suit had been discarded for a simple cotton frock. The artfully shadowed makeup had been washed away. The ultrasmart, glittering facade was gone. There was a wholesome outdoor look about her now—a look of sailing boats and green hills and open country roads.

"Better or worse?"

"Better," I said. "Much better."

"Don't you like high fashion?"

"Not when it's designed to make females look like poles or balloons. Or the ballyhoo that makes an entire wardrobe obsolete four times a year."

"That's the wrong attitude, Scott. Fashion changes keep money circulating. Think of all the employment it creates—mills weaving new fabrics, seamstresses working overtime, truck drivers making deliveries, salespeople, models, copywriters, everybody."

In a wacky kind of way it made sense. "I see your point. Can I help you pack?"

"Sure. Close that suitcase."

I had to kneel on the lid to get it locked. "How about our cocktails?"

"Later. I'm dining with the family and Adam said to ask you along. He wants to tell us about the book—the one they sold to the movies. Would you close the trunk, too?"

I swung the two sections together. "Were you frightened at finding a strange man in the apartment this morning?"

"Petrified."

"Do I look like a housebreaker?"

"I don't know. Jimmy Valentine and Raffles were supposed to be very charming."

I grinned. "Talking about crooks reminds me of your ex-husband. Did you know that his girl friend is missing, too?"

She turned to stare at me. "Kate Wallace?"

I nodded. "Left her job and apparently the city."

"She's with Dan?"

"Seems likely."

"Poor girl." Barbara sighed and returned to her chores. "She's due for a rude awakening."

"No resentment?"

"None at all. The only person I resent in all this blue-eyed world is my stepmother. Would you call the desk, Scott, please, and ask them to send up a couple of bellboys?"

I complied. There was mild confusion for a couple of minutes when the boys arrived and wrestled their load onto a hand cart. Barbara took a final critical look around and we vacated the room. The trunk would follow along by express, but we got the suitcases into a cab, and for the second time that day I headed toward Varney's apartment.

The prescription was perfect.

A properly chilled martini lightly kissed by vermouth. I mixed the ingredients myself. It heightened the bloom on Barbara's face and helped her to relax. She had unpacked her bags and made a quick tour of the apartment, tossing things in a carton. In a matter of minutes, the place seemed brighter and airier. Now she sat on the sofa with her legs folded under her.

"I'm surprised Dan didn't try to sell the furniture," she said.

"Too risky. He wanted to get away quickly, without arousing suspicion."

We were waiting for Adam and the Dodds to pick us up.

"How's your father?" I asked.

Pain shadowed her eyes. "He's low, very low."

"Did you see him?"

"Only for an instant. Lorraine had gone down for some coffee and he was alone. But he didn't recog-

nize me. He was lying so still, in a coma, sort of."
She hugged herself as though suddenly chilled.
"What a dreadful ending! Dad would want us near
him at a time like this. If it weren't for Lorraine I
might be able to...to...." She tightened her lips
to keep them from trembling.

"How long since you've spoken to him?"

"It seems like ages. Ironic, isn't it? Who do you
think introduced dad to Lorraine?"

I waited in silence.

"Me. I brought her home from school one weekend. We went to the University of Wisconsin
together. Did you know that?"

I shook my head.

"Lorraine was older, senior when I was a fresh-
man, and something of a campus beauty. I was flat-
tered, I suppose, at her interest in me. I realize now
that she wanted to see New York and how she
maneuvered the invitation."

"And your father took to her?"

"Naturally. She was so young and desirable. She
had a lovely figure and she played her cards so
cleverly. Poor dad. He thought he was recapturing
his youth. He took us to a theater and a supper club
and danced all night. I felt like a third wheel, a
stranger. Then, a couple of weeks later, she came to
New York alone, took a hotel room and phoned
him. Dad was delighted. He courted her outrageously. And after that he kept inviting her back, at his
expense. He was moonstruck, hopelessly in love."

"The dangerous age," I said. "Falling in love
after sixty can be an emotional blockbuster."

"It was more than that. He built a false image of
himself. She made him feel young, dashing, virile. It

was all new to dad, something he had never before experienced. Never had the time for. He's a self-made man, you know."

I nodded. Barbara huddled back on the sofa. She seemed under a compulsion, as if talking it out had some kind of cathartic effect.

"The hotels were his life. Dad worked eighteen hours a day, building the chain. He neglected his wife and his family and his health. We hardly got to see him. He was always moving from city to city. And then he got his first heart attack and the doctors threw a real scare into him. Retire, they told him, or take the consequences. He had no choice. But meanwhile mother had died and now he had too much time on his hands, nothing to keep him occupied. That's when Lorraine appeared. Vickie and I were disturbed, but Adam only laughed. He isn't laughing now."

I said nothing.

"Lorraine gave dad a new lease on life. And after he married her she tried to cancel the lease. She didn't seem to care about his health. She was selfish and inconsiderate. She led him a wild chase, traveling, parties, late hours, all deliberately planned, and poor dad struggling to keep pace with her. There was nothing we could do. Adam had already fought with dad and we were all barred from the house." Barbara's eyes were suddenly brimming. "Of course it had to end in . . . in disaster. . . ."

I looked away and when I turned back her eyes were dry again.

She managed a small and rueful smile. "Is there anything left in the martini shaker?"

"Yes."

"May I get you another?"

"Please." I pointed to the desk. "I didn't quite finish my search this morning. Mind if I take another look?"

"Help yourself."

I went back to the bottom drawer. There was a large accumulation of newspaper clippings, all book reviews. Varney probably had his eye out for new authors. There was a full-page photograph of Barbara, torn from *Vogue*, showing her at the fountain in Riverside Park near the yacht basin. There was an advertisement offering to sell a month's supply of vitamins, minerals and a happy quantity of royal jelly. I was stuffing it all back when the doorbell rang.

Barbara called out from the pantry, "Answer that, Scott, will you, please?"

I went to the door and opened it.

A bulky man loomed over the threshold. His long, ill-fitting coat was open and he wore no hat on a grizzled skull. His thin lips had a bitter cast and his red-veined eyes glittered recklessly.

The gun in his hand was a .38-caliber revolver and he kept its unblinking eye aimed square at my chest.

7

HE SPOKE IN A harsh voice, with a thick and pronounced Scottish burr.

"Step bock, ye domned crook!"

I did not argue. For me, this apartment seemed jinxed. Twice in one day I had opened the door on a packet of trouble. I backed away and he followed me into the room, walking stiff-kneed, with an awkward limp. The smell of raw whiskey hung heavily in the air around him. He kicked the door shut, glowering ferociously.

"So ye finally sneaked bock. Ye came home, Varney. By God, I've been waitin' for this." His jaw muscles lumped whitely. "Where's my money, ye swundler? My two hundred thousand dollars."

The question identified him. The Scotsman was Fred Duncan, the man whose book had been sold to the movies. He stood with his square-toed shoes apart, drunk and baleful. The gun seemed to be a part of him, an extension of his inner venom.

"Take it easy," I said. "You're making a mistake, Duncan."

"So ye know who I am. Well, Mr. Varney, this is no mistake. No mistake at all. My lawyer tells me ye collected the money and disappeared."

"I am not Varney," I told him quietly.

"Then who are ye? A stranger waitin' for a trolley, I suppose. Here by accident, answerin' Varney's bell. It won't wash, Varney. I want my money."

"If you'll just listen for a moment, Duncan—"

"No more listenin'. I listened long enough to my lawyer and all I get are excuses. It takes time, he says. We have to sue, he says. First we have to get a judgment and then we have to collect the judgment. But he's wrong, Varney. I dinna have to wait for no courts to give me a judgment."

We heard an audible gasp and I turned.

Barbara stood in the pantry door, her eyes round and transfixed by the sight of a gun. Her fingers were clasped in a bowknot of distress at her throat.

Duncan took a limping step backward. The gun described a short arc to include Barbara.

"All right, lady. Stond over there, close to Varney. Are you his wife?"

She swallowed hugely. Her lips moved for a moment before she got them wired for sound. "No." There was a sudden indignation in her voice. "And this man is not Dan Varney."

Duncan sneered. "It's no good, lady. Ye canna protect him. He's a plunderin' thief."

"Of course." She stood erect now, facing up to him. "I agree with you. Dan Varney is a thief. But not this man. This man is a lawyer and he came here to look for Varney."

"A lawyer?" His brows had contracted into a scowl.

"Yes. Scott Jordan. I'm sure your own lawyer must have mentioned his name."

It rang a bell. He studied me with the narrow-lidded shrewdness of a drunk. "Scott Jordan, hey?"

"Would you like proof?" I asked. I started to reach, but my hand stopped in midair at his sudden growl.

He was not drunk enough to be incautious. He told me to pull my coat open very slowly. He saw no shoulder holster, no gun butt projecting from my waistband. He instructed me to withdraw the wallet with my fingertips. I followed his suggestions to the letter. A simple twitch of his trigger finger could send eternity hurtling at me with muzzle velocity.

"All right," he said. "Toss it on the coffee table."

I did so. He limped over, dumped its contents and separated them with one hand. There were professional cards, credit cards and registration cards, enough to keep me from being locked up as a vagrant. Duncan glanced at them and then straightened, a vinegar twist on his lips.

"So you're the lawyer who's blockin' payment."

"No, sir. I'm the lawyer who's trying to expedite payment."

"What's that?" He looked puzzled.

"Didn't Birnbaum tell you? I represent Coleman and I'm trying to protect his interests. It was Varney who stole your money. I want to find him and get it back."

"Birnbaum says they're both responsible."

"Legally, yes."

"Then why the hell are you fightin' the case?" he said with a flash of anger. "I dinna care who pays. Varney's missin'. Let Coleman get it up."

"He can't. Coleman hasn't got two hundred thousand dollars."

Duncan had the look of a man whose veins were nourished by some corrosive acid rather than blood.

"I want what's comin' to me," he said fiercely. "From either partner or both. And I mean to get it one way or another."

He glared balefully, then turned without another word, and limped toward the door. What he had hoped to accomplish by this mission, I couldn't say. Perhaps he was constitutionally unable to sit still and wait for the courts to take their slow and ponderous course. Goaded by frustration and fortified with alcohol, some action seemed indicated. He was hoping, perhaps, that the sight of a gun would terrify Varney and accelerate a settlement.

The door closed behind him.

Barbara emptied her lungs with a heartfelt sigh. She sank back against a nest of pillows on the sofa, limp with relief. "Good Lord!" she breathed.

"Amen."

"Was that gun really loaded?"

"Yes, indeed."

She shuddered. "It—it looked so deadly."

"It was designed for death."

She compressed her lips. "They should never have been invented."

"Then we'd have to go back to using shillelaghs and slingshots. Very inefficient. How can civilization destroy itself with such obsolete weapons?"

"Scott. You sound pessimistic."

"That's one of the hazards of reading newspapers."

"Well, I don't like it."

"I don't like it either."

"And besides, that man is a menace. Shouldn't we call the police?"

"Not this time. He was grievously wronged and more than a little drunk. Let's give him a break."

A buzzer sounded. There was an intercom system between each apartment and the downstairs hall. Barbara got up and I heard her address the contrivance.

She came back. "It's Adam. Vickie and Gil are with him and they're waiting in a cab."

8

DINNER THAT EVENING was not a festive occasion.

First they were subdued because of M. Parker Coleman's illness, and then appalled at Barbara's account of Fred Duncan's intrusion with a gun.

"Good heavens!" Gil Dodd said. "The man's unstable. He may try for Adam next."

Victoria nodded. "I insist we notify the police."

"It won't happen again," I assured her.

"Can you guarantee that? Adam's life may be in danger."

"Don't worry about it," Adam said. "I'll be careful."

They resumed nibbling at their food in an apathetic and half-hearted manner. In time, the waiter cleared away and brought coffee.

"I'd like to know more about Duncan," I told Adam. "If the family won't be bored."

They protested simultaneously. Adam's problems were of mutual concern. They were deeply interested.

"And besides," Victoria said, "Gil is full of ideas. He may have some useful suggestions."

Adam lit a cigarette and leaned back. "I told you that he worked at the Merchant's Trust."

"That's your bank, isn't it, Adam?"

"Yes."

"How come? There's no branch near your office."

"Well, dad has always banked at the Merchant's Trust. He's one of their most important depositors. So they make concessions to members of the family—no minimum balance, that sort of thing. In a tight operation like ours, it sometimes helps."

"All right. And you said he used to be a cop."

"Yes. A detective third grade attached to the Homicide Bureau of the District Attorney's office. His book contains disclosures he learned while working in that capacity. He had the inside dope on a shocking incident that's been a mystery for years. He wrote The Kingpins out of need and bitterness. His whole personality has been soured by the crippling shot that got him pensioned off the force and landed him in the basement of a bank as the safe-deposit custodian."

"And these revelations induced the movie sale."

"Yes. Remember the Albert Jaekel case?"

"Which one? Jaekel was involved in a hundred cases."

"I'm referring to a charge of homicide. The murder of a union organizer. Jaekel had been indicted by the Grand Jury and they had him cold, an eyewitness ready to testify, the works."

"And the eyewitness conveniently died."

"That's right. A man named Ben Keller. Fell out of a window in the Crescent Hotel."

I cocked a skeptical eyebrow. "Fell?"

"Yes. Fell. After he was pushed."

Even though it happened some years back, a lot of people would remember the case.

Albert Jaekel. Hoodlum and torpedo. A slum-bred

immigrant, tough, cynical, ruthless, consumed by ambition. Street fighter and official executioner. No job too small or too mean. A racketeer who clawed and bludgeoned his way to the top. Until at last he had the whole Brooklyn waterfront in his pocket from its stevedores to its billion-dollar shipping interests.

Albert Jaekel. Possessed of one really remarkable talent.

With a hundred lines out to land him, he always managed to throw the hook. Except once. A single year spent in a federal pen on charges of income-tax evasion. Bribery, duplicity, violence and murder had aided him in cheating the electric chair.

But all that was behind him now. Jaekel had no more problems—and no more luxuries, either. No more fourteen-room mansions. His new address was a narrow mahogany box planted six feet down with a granite tombstone marking the spot. His career had been concluded, ironically enough, in a shoe-shine parlor. Seven bullets from two automatics had stopped the clock for Albert Jaekel.

His spirit, whatever its destination, was more likely manipulating a pitchfork than playing a harp.

But curiosity and the foul taste of corruption lingered on. People still wonder about Ben Keller, the eyewitness against Jaekel on a murder charge, the one time they had him cold, wrapped up and ready for delivery to Sing Sing. The D.A.'s office had taken Keller into protective custody. They held him incommunicado at the Crescent Hotel. Detectives from the Homicide Bureau kept him under constant surveillance twenty-four hours around the clock.

And yet, somehow, inexplicably, shortly before

the trial, key witness Keller had plunged screaming through the window of his room. They found his lifeless body on the pavement below, his tongue silenced, the prosecution scuttled.

Not for an instant did anyone believe that Ben Keller had committed suicide. For the man had been eager to sing in order to save his hide.

Which left only one alternative.

Murder!

Yet how could a man be dispatched behind locked doors in a guarded room?

The inference was odious. Bribery, wholesale corruption, police contamination.

I looked at Adam. "Duncan reveals the inside story of what happened that night at the Crescent Hotel?"

"Yes. Thinly disguised as fiction."

"Can he prove it?"

"He was there at the time, on duty with the District Attorney's squad, assigned to the detail guarding Keller."

I pursed my lips in a silent whistle. Even at this late date it would cause a furor. Proof of police corruption would shatter public confidence. The governor's hand would be forced. A new investigation might be ordered. The boom would be lowered and heads would roll.

I said, "All you have is Duncan's own version. Is that enough for a movie company? Those boys like to play it safe. They're especially vulnerable to lawsuits for libel and slander. Some of the detectives involved may still be on the public payroll. Suppose Zenith invests a million dollars on a picture and then somebody slaps them with an injunction."

"They understand all that. They've changed names, places, dates. There's a hell of a movie involved in this story, Scott, and they're willing to risk it. They've got a built-in audience of seventy million people who remember the case. And if anyone starts a lawsuit, Duncan will come into court and blow the lid off. That's in his contract."

"Now, look," Gil Dodd exclaimed. "The suspense is killing. What really happened to Keller?"

Adam looked at him and shrugged. "There are damn few saints in the Police Department. In any organization that size, you can always find a few men for sale at the right price. The percentage is small, thank God, but it's there. I doubt if Jaekel had to probe for a soft spot. A man in his position would know who could be reached. It would have to be someone in authority, someone who could distribute the payoff and manipulate the personnel. I can't guess how much it cost. The total must have been fantastic. Under the circumstances, Jaekel wouldn't quibble. After all, his life was at stake."

Adam's two sisters and his brother-in-law were listening as if mesmerized.

"What happened was simple enough. The money was paid and two of Jaekel's hatchet men got access to Keller's room. The usual weapons, of course, were out. No artillery, no switchblade, no blunt instrument. And so the window was a perfect alternative and just as effective. The whole operation was over in a matter of seconds and the two assassins were gone before Keller's body hit the pavement."

Barbara shivered.

"At the time, Duncan was off duty in an adjoining room. He swears he heard Keller scream: 'No...no...don't...please....' He says he ran to his door and opened it and saw two men, strangers, hurrying away. He saw the sergeant in charge standing there, making no move to stop them.''

"Did Duncan get a piece of the bribe?" I asked.

"He says no."

"Yet he kept silent all this time. Why didn't he open up when the investigation started?"

"I asked him that. He told me a man named Strobe—Ernie Strobe—was in charge of the detail. A despotic, arbitrary martinet, always pulling his rank. Duncan was afraid to cross him. He knew instinctively what had happened and he wanted to stay clear. He had an invalid wife at the time and he needed his job, so he kept his lips sealed.''

"Afraid of a police sergeant?" Gil Dodd said.

"And afraid of Albert Jaekel, too."

I understood Fred Duncan's position. How could he talk? The long arm of Jaekel's vengeance had been vividly demonstrated before his eyes that night in the Crescent Hotel. With paralyzing regularity every witness against Jaekel had lost the use of his tongue, had disappeared from sight or been cut down in cold blood. Duncan was only a cop, near the bottom of the ladder. Why be quixotic? Why risk his security or his life?

"And now he's no longer afraid," I said.

"For three reasons. Jaekel is dead. Duncan is no longer on the force. And he wants money very badly."

"When did you first meet him?"

"Some months ago at the bank. I had filled out an application for a safe-deposit box and he saw my occupation, literary agent. He told me he was writing a book and wanted to know if I'd read it when he finished."

"He never met Varney at all?"

"Never. Although they may have spoken on the phone once or twice."

"That accent of Duncan's. . . ." I shook my head.

"A lulu, isn't it? He came to this country as a boy and it never left him."

Victoria Dodd looked at her watch and said, "It's getting late. We'll miss visiting hours at the hospital."

Gil Dodd was on his feet at once, signaling for a check. I pushed my chair back and helped Barbara with her coat.

Adam said, "Why not come along, Scott? We'll probably be stuck in the waiting room anyway, and if you have any more questions. . . ."

Barbara seconded the invitation, so I tagged after them.

One of the prerogatives of great wealth is medical care with style and elegance. St. John's was the ultimate in hospital architecture, an antiseptic pile of white limestone towering majestically over the East River. For the carriage trade there was a new wing, furnished in Danish modern.

But the instant we stepped out of the elevator, I knew something was wrong.

The floor nurse rose precipitately. She advanced to intercept us, a look of professional sympathy lengthening her face. At that moment a doctor emerged from one of the rooms. Tall, gray-templed, immaculate in his starched white jacket, he swerved toward us, waving the nurse back.

A foreboding hush settled over the group, as if some telepathic message made his words unnecessary.

"I'm sorry. We did everything we could."

"He's gone," Adam said numbly.

Barbara whimpered and looked stricken. Victoria went pale and swayed. Gil Dodd steadied her with a protective arm.

"When did it happen?" Adam asked.

"About fifteen minutes ago."

"Can we see him?"

The doctor shook his head. "Not now, Adam." As the old man's physician he was probably acquainted with family details. "The widow's in there with him. We'll get her out in a moment."

I felt out of place. At a time like this I knew the family wanted to be alone. I murmured some words and faded unobtrusively back toward the elevators.

9

THE FUNERAL WAS HELD on Thursday and by noon M. Parker Coleman had been interred in Woodlawn Cemetery. At the services the widow sat apart from the rest of the family, heavily veiled in black. Hiding what on her face, I wondered. A look of satisfaction or the ravages of grief?

I did not follow the cortege. To me, the embalmed remains bear no relation to a living memory, and the finality of watching a coffin lowered into the earth is a pagan ritual, cruel and racking to the survivors.

Both the *Times* and the *News* had allotted the deceased about six inches of column on the obituary page. A photograph taken some years earlier, about the time he'd been a client of my old employer, showed him in the familiar pose, the traplike mouth clamped tight over a stubborn jaw. Metallic hair was combed sideways to cover a flattish skull. His genes had left their vigorous engraving on Victoria Dodd, somewhat less on Adam, and not at all on Barbara.

The family had drawn together in a tight unit, keeping themselves isolated. Barbara, I learned, was temporarily staying at the Dodds' apartment.

Max Turner had called several times to report

only negative results. No passport had been issued, no flight ticket sold in Varney's name. I told him to keep hunting.

On Friday morning I received a call from Fred Duncan's lawyer. "Irving Birnbaum, Counselor. You don't remember me, do you?"

"The name sounds familiar," I said, "but I can't seem to place it."

"That's because you never come to class reunions. Skinny guy with mustache and glasses two rows ahead of you in Torts."

It came back to me through the years in a hazy kaleidoscope of memory. "No," I said. "It can't be. Not the man with the notebook."

"The same." He seemed pleased at my recollection.

The haze dispelled itself. I remembered Birnbaum as a slight chap, very intense, very studious, with a remarkable facility in shorthand that permitted him to copy an entire lecture verbatim. At night he would transcribe his notes and they were always available to anyone who missed a class or needed a brushup.

"First time our paths have crossed out of school," he said. "But I occasionally read about your exploits."

"Those newspapers. They exaggerate."

"Look, Jordan. I want to thank you on behalf of my client."

"For what?"

"He was up here yesterday and he dropped a hint about that incident with the gun. I managed to worm the story out of him. It was mighty decent of you not to call the law."

"He didn't know what he was doing. He was tanked."

"I understand. Thanks anyway." He cleared his throat. "Incidentally, I received your notice of appearance and answer in the Coleman suit. A general denial, Counselor?" His tone was gently chiding.

"That's our defense."

"And very flimsy. Zenith Films paid the money to Coleman's firm. Let him deduct his ten percent and pay the rest to my client."

"Don't you know about Varney?"

"Varney is not our problem. Under the law, partners are equally responsible. You know that, Jordan. I'm afraid we'll have to move for summary judgment."

"What good is a judgment if you can't collect? Adam Coleman hasn't got anywhere near two hundred thousand dollars."

"I understand he's going to inherit a bundle from his father's estate."

"Who told you that?"

"Duncan."

"He's wrong. So far as I know the old man drew a will disinheriting all his children. Why not hold off a little? Give me a chance to find Varney and force him to make restitution."

"If there's anything left."

"There will be if we can catch him soon enough. And I've got some private detectives working on it."

"How long will it take?"

"I can't say."

"My client is a very impatient man, as you probably know."

"I had a firsthand demonstration," I said wryly. "But you admit I did him a favor."

"Yes."

"Will you let him do one for me?"

"What kind of favor?"

"I'd like a chat with him."

"Well, now...."

"Wait a minute before you object. I know this is highly irregular. But there may be some repercussions on that book of his. If it's filmed there's going to be a lot of publicity. A number of people will be affected. It's going to open a lot of old wounds. I'd like to question Duncan about it."

"He's a tough nut to crack." Birnbaum was wavering. "I'm not sure he'll talk to you."

"Let me try."

"You won't compromise his case against Coleman in any way?"

"I give you my word."

"And you'll stick to the subject matter in his book?"

"Religiously."

"All right. But only because you didn't blow the whistle on him after that gun episode."

We made the usual polite remarks about lunch in the near future and hung up. Almost immediately the phone rang again.

"Scott? Adam." His voice was strained, on edge. "Can you be at my office in an hour?"

"What's up?"

"Somebody's coming and I want you here when he arrives."

"Who?"

"A policeman, Sergeant Ernie Strobe."

"You mentioned him once before. Isn't he the cop who was in charge of the detail assigned to guard Ben Keller that night in the Crescent Hotel?"

"Yes."

"What's he after?"

"I don't know. But I had a call from Zenith Films this morning. They say he threatened to file an injunction if they start filming the Duncan book."

"I'll be there," I said.

Adam rang off. I sat for a moment, pondering the coincidence. Permission to chat with Fred Duncan had come just in time. I told Cassidy my two destinations and headed first toward the Merchant's Trust.

A glass facade, vast and gleaming, afforded passersby a striking view of the bank's interior. The atmosphere was dignified and hushed, with polite tellers, polite guards, and a phalanx of polite vice-presidents regimentally arrayed at polished desks behind a brass railing. One of the guards directed me to a marble stairway that descended to the vaults on a lower level.

Down here, insulated from the world, was an echoing, tomblike silence. Heavy, stainless-steel bars fortified the vault area. Behind them, row upon row of safe-deposit boxes were visible, and at a small desk I could see the custodian, Fred Duncan.

He heard my footsteps, rose automatically and limped forward, the grim face dour and preoccupied. He turned a key and swung the door on its soundless hinges. "Yes, sir."

I entered and the door closed. He turned to the desk for a signature slip. Then he looked up and recognized me. His face lost all expression, like a man filling a royal flush.

"Good morning, Duncan," I said pleasantly.

He was cold sober, eyes clear and narrowed suspiciously.

"Can you spare me a few minutes?" I asked.

"What do ye want?"

"I'd like a word with you."

"Ye have no business here," he said harshly. He limped to the door and pulled it open. "Out."

"Look, Duncan—"

"Out."

I shook my head and stayed put. "I want to rent a safe-deposit box."

Seamed lips flattened against his teeth. "Why here?"

"Why not here? It's a good bank, isn't it? Solvent, respectable, a member of the Federal Reserve System, convenient to my office. There are boxes available, I assume."

His stare was coldly hostile and searching. After a moment he shrugged, sat down at the desk, produced an application card and uncapped a pen. I answered his questions and watched him record the information.

"What size box?" he demanded finally.

"The smallest."

"Nine dollars and ninety cents." His Scottish burr had thickened. "Payable in advance."

I counted out the exact sum. He turned the card around and handed me the pen for a specimen signature. I wrote my name. He checked a card index for available boxes, found an envelope with a pair of keys and limped to the vault wall. The two keys opened a small brass compartment. He withdrew a narrow rectangular box. Without comment, grimly silent, he led the way to a row of doors and pulled one open.

The small cubicle was occupied. A slight bookkeeper-type man looked up, startled. His hand, poised midway to his mouth, held a half-consumed sandwich. A container of coffee was on the table. An open safe-deposit box contained salt and pepper shakers.

Well, I thought, why not? Restaurants in the midtown area are crowded during lunch hour. Where else could he find privacy and quiet for his noontime nourishment?

"Oh, excuse me," Duncan said and closed the door.

He shook his head in irritation and tried the next cubicle. It was empty. He snapped the light, placed the strongbox on a table, handed me one of the two keys, and closed the door.

It sealed me off in an isolation chamber that locked from the inside. Here, deep under the roaring city, was total seclusion. A Mecca for the periodic pilgrimmage of coupon clippers, a temple for the tycoon to audit his holdings, for the tax evader to fondle his cash, for the courtesan to admire her gems, for the minor executive on a tight budget to eat his homemade lunch.

I found some innocuous papers in my pocket and dropped them into the box. Duncan would hear them sliding around in case he shook it. I waited briefly, giving him time to get used to this new development. After a moment, I closed the box and carried it out.

Duncan accepted it without expression. He had left the compartment door open. Now he slid the box into its waiting space. He held his hand out for the key. I gave it to him. Each compartment is secured by two separate locks. The key to one of them is retained by the bank and the customer's key operates the other. Duncan used them both and returned mine to me.

"We're running into a little trouble, Duncan," I said.

He had no comment.

"It concerns your book *The Kingpins*. Somebody threatened to file an injunction against Zenith Films."

He stirred uneasily. He moistened his lips. "What for?"

"To prevent their filming the story."

"Who?"

"Ernie Strobe."

A white ring appeared around his bleak mouth.

"Zenith sent out some publicity puffs on the picture," I said. "Apparently Strobe heard about it and he's moving in."

Strobe's name evoked memories. Duncan stood stolidly and then moved his shoulders in a fatalistic shrug.

"Are you standing pat on your story?" I asked.

"Ay."

"Strobe made an appointment to see Coleman."

"What guid will it do him?"

"I don't know. But I want to protect your interests."

"Ha!"

"You want to collect your two hundred thousand dollars, don't you?"

"Ay."

"That would depend on the validity of your sale to Zenith Films. They bought the rights to your book on a warranty of truth. And now Ernie Strobe has threatened to enjoin them from making the picture."

"On what grounds?"

"Libel, slander, defamation of character. If he prevails, if Zenith is stuck with a property they can't film, they may demand their money back. And in that case, your action against Coleman will collapse. You'll never be able to collect from anybody."

He stood, brooding. Gloom haunted his face. His eyes sought mine. "What do ye suggest, Muster Jordan."

"An affidavit," I said. "Just to be on the safe side. I'd like you to swear to the truth of the statements in your book."

"Will that help?"

"I'm not sure. At any rate, I'd like your sworn statement on paper."

"Shouldn't I discuss this with Birnbaum feerst?"

"Absolutely. I don't expect you to sign it without his permission. Suppose I write it out, then you can read it to him on the phone, and if he says okay, you can sign it."

He found a sheet of paper and I sat at the desk and started to write:

State of New York, County of New York.

Fred Duncan, being duly sworn, deposes and says. . . .

It was a simple affirmation that the facts surrounding the death of Ben Keller as described in his book were true, and that he personally had been a witness.

Duncan read it and said, "Not necessary to call Birnbaum aboot this."

"Is there a notary public in the bank?"

"Upstairs."

"Can you get away for a couple of minutes?"

He nodded and called for a temporary substitute. I accompanied him to the main floor. One of the tellers was a notary and attested Duncan's signature. When the formalities were completed, I offered him my hand.

He gave it a brief and grudging shake.

10

A STENCIL ON THE DOOR said: Coleman & Varney, Literary Agents.

If the business survived, Adam would probably shorten the firm name. He was pacing restlessly when I entered. It was the first time I had seen him since the funeral and his face was lined and tired. He threw his hands wide in a distracted gesture and let out a groan.

"I swear, Scott, I don't know which way to turn."

"Sit down," I said. I watched him sink bonelessly into a chair. "Tell me about it."

"First Zenith called and then Strobe. He said Keller's death was a suicide. He said if anybody makes a picture claiming otherwise, he'll prevent them from showing it."

"He can try. That doesn't mean his injunction will be granted."

"Why not?"

"Zenith will claim the story is fiction, that it does not portray real people."

"You're wrong, Scott. That's just the point. They're touting *The Kingpins* as a true exposé of police corruption. That's why the story appealed to them. That's why they bought it."

"*Caveat emptor.*"

He gave me a puzzled look.

"Let the buyer beware," I said. "Zenith nego-
tiated for the property with their eyes open."

"Granted. But they're entitled to Duncan's cooperation. They may need his testimony."

"He's available."

"Will he play ball, though? Suppose he refuses to
testify unless he gets his money."

"Don't worry about it. Duncan wants to protect
his interests and he'll be so advised by his own
lawyer."

Adam rumpled his hair. "Are you sure Zenith
can't renege on this deal, can't demand their money
back?"

"The contracts have been signed, sealed and delivered and the money paid."

"Have you ever seen a movie contract, Scott? It's
quite a document. You need a microscope for the
small print, and don't expect to find any loopholes.
Another thing—"

Adam turned as the outer door opened. He
peered into the anteroom. "Sergeant Strobe?" he
said. "I've been expecting you. In here, sir."

I had built a preconceived image of the man and
he almost met specifications. He had great sloping
shoulders and a graying leonine head. His face was
craggy, with liverish patches under glacially cold
eyes. He carried himself with a kind of domineering
assurance. His dark suit was no ready-to-wear gar-
ment.

He spread his feet and said, "Let's get the names
straight. Which one is Coleman and which is
Varney?"

"I'm Coleman," Adam said. "Mr. Varney is out of town."

"And him?" A blunt thumb stabbed in my direction.

"Scott Jordan, my attorney."

He gave me a look of stony appraisal. "Haven't I seen you around the courts, Counselor?"

"Probably."

"Are you here by design or coincidence?"

"Design. Mr. Coleman requested my presence."

"You're his lawyer?"

"That's right."

"Any idea why I'm here?"

"Suppose you tell us."

"Your client handled the sale of a manuscript to Zenith Films. I want to see a copy."

"Any special reason?"

"Damn right, Counselor. From what I hear, that story is an alleged inside account of the Keller incident. I understand it repudiates the official version, that Keller committed suicide. Let me tell you something, gentlemen. I was there at the time. On the spot. I spoke to Keller an hour before he died. That monkey was a gutless, blubbery wreck, scared witless."

"What's your point?"

"Just this. He was afraid to testify against Albert Jaekel and he was afraid to cross the District Attorney. He stood to lose either way. If Jaekel was acquitted, he'd go after Keller and put him in cold storage. If Jaekel got convicted, his organization would do the job. A squealer would never be allowed to live. And if Keller refused to testify, the D.A. would peel his hide. They already had his statement in writing.''

"So?"

"Can't you see it, man? He wouldn't even eat his dinner that night. He was jumpy, damn near incoherent. I think he had his nose-dive already planned. Why eat? He'd be dead in an hour anyway.''

"Did you suspect that?'' I asked.

"All right. Maybe I should have guessed and taken precautions. None of us is infallible. I caught my hell from the D.A. at the time. From the Deputy Chief Inspector and the Commissioner, too. They put every man-jack on that detail through the wringer. They grilled us front, back, and sideways. And what did they find? Nothing off-color. Not one damn thing out of focus.''

"A whitewash,'' I said. "To protect the department.''

Blood flushed through his face. He folded his arms across his chest. "It was suicide, mister. Plain and simple. But there's always somebody looking for an angle. Now, years later, Duncan sees a chance to make himself a wad. He may have to assassinate a couple of reputations, but what the hell! He's got two hundred thousand dollars riding on the lie.''

"Have you discussed this with a lawyer?''

"Not yet. That's why I want to see the manuscript. I want to know exactly what it says.''

"I'm afraid I can't help you,'' Adam said.

"What do you mean?''

"I just don't have a copy available.''

Strobe bent stiffly forward, squinting at him. "You mean there is none?''

"Yes, there is. But it's in Philadelphia, being considered by a publisher who's interested in a movie tie-in. And Zenith Films has a copy."

The liverish patches darkened. Strobe shifted his gaze to me. "Zenith can't afford to make that picture, Counselor."

"They can't afford not to," I said. "They've already invested two hundred thousand dollars."

"They'll be stuck with the prints. It'll never be shown if I go to court."

"You may delay them with litigation. But they'll win if they can show the story is true."

"How? By whose testimony? Duncan's? The damn Scotchman knows he's lying and they'll never get him on the witness stand."

"He has no choice," I said. "He'll have to testify to protect his own interests."

"You think he'll stick to that story under oath?"

"He can't help himself. He gave me a sworn affidavit this morning."

Strobe dropped his arms. He stood for a moment, flexing his fingers. His eyes burned in a face swollen tight with anger. He opened his mouth to speak, thought better of it, turned abruptly and headed for the door. The cylinder closed it behind him with a sinister hiss.

Adam exhaled. "My God! That bird gives me the willies."

I agreed with him. You could sense a hard core of ruthless cynicism in the man. He radiated brutality. Ernie Strobe had missed his calling. He would make a fine commissar of public safety for some dictator.

"What do you make of it, Scott?" Adam asked.

"He's worried. Duncan's story may spark a fresh

investigation. It's possible that other men from that detail are retired now, no longer under Strobe's domination. One of them may reverse his field under pressure.''

"All the characters in that book are disguised,'' Adam said. "For example, the cop on top is named Sergeant Light and—''

I stopped him, frowning. "Wait a minute. Do you know anything about photography?''

"Not much.''

"There's a device that eliminates the need for flashbulbs. It's called a strobe light. I wonder if Duncan was playing cute. He may have used the name of Sergeant Light as a thin disguise for Sergeant Strobe.''

Adam grimaced. "Isn't that too close for comfort?''

"Offhand, I'd say yes. I suggest you get in touch with Zenith Films and have them change the character's name.''

Adam nodded. He looked thoughtful. "Duncan never mentioned the size of the payoff. I wonder how much Strobe got?''

"Plenty. He probably enjoys the authority of being a cop or else he'd retire.'' I paused. "What's eating Duncan? What makes him so avid for money? Isn't his pension from the department and his job at the bank enough to support him?''

"Yes. But he has other obligations.''

"The invalid wife?''

"No. She died some years ago. But Duncan also had a son.'' Adam shook his head sympathetically.

"Go on,'' I prompted.

"The son was killed by a hit-and-run driver. Left

a widow and two kids. They never traced the car and the widow never collected a dime. They're too proud to go on relief and Duncan's helping to support them. That's why he wrote the book. He hoped it would sell and make some money. He wanted the money for his grandchildren, get them off on a decent start."

The picture of Fred Duncan began to focus. I had a more lucid understanding of the man now, and of his motives. At his age a man begins to contemplate the past, to sit in judgment, to assess the score. What had he accomplished? Very little. And yet it had not been a total waste. Those grandchildren were symbols of his immortality. His one chance for the future. This time, perhaps, it would have meaning. And money could help. The two hundred thousand dollars had been a windfall, the once-in-a-lifetime stroke of fortune.

And Varney had robbed him.

Had robbed the kids, too.

It explained his obsession and bitterness. He wanted that money, and its source was immaterial. And he was prepared to tangle with Sergeant Ernie Strobe if necessary.

"How long is the manuscript?" I asked.

"Seventy thousand words. He must have sweated blood getting it down on paper. I understand his daughter-in-law helped him with the typing."

"Do you remember her name?"

"Yes. Ruth Duncan." He glanced at his watch. "It's almost time for lunch. How about a bite with me?"

I had a sudden thought. "Not today, Adam. I'm taking a run upstate."

"Where to?"

"A town called Ormont."

"What the devil for?"

"Kate Wallace's people live there. I want to speak to them. After all, she disappeared about the same time Varney did. They may have some idea where she went."

11

I DROVE UP THE TACONIC. The noonday sun burned overhead in a cloudless sky. A riot of color flung itself impressionistically across the countryside. Red maples, silver birches, and balsams covered the foothills in a vast umbrella.

The northward stream of traffic was light and I kept the tappets clicking at a steady sixty. The curving blacktop unraveled and sang under the Buick's tires. I had checked a map and was watching the parkway exits with their picturesque and historical names. The turnoff came suddenly and I swung the wheel hard, tires screeching protestingly at the sharp change in direction.

The county road dipped and tilted into a valley. Near the tip of its western rim, Ormont dozed sluggishly in the heat. Its main street was two blocks long. I stopped off at a drugstore for a sandwich and directions to the Wallace home.

It was a white frame structure on a sun-parched lawn. A green awning shielded the front door. I climbed two steps and rang the bell. A vacuum cleaner was droning noisily behind the door and I rang again, holding the button.

The noise stopped and a moment later the door opened. A motherly type with pleasant eyes and a comfortable bosom smiled at me and said, "Yes?"

I handed her a card.

She read aloud. "Scott Jordan, Attorney-at-Law. My goodness—Don't tell me I'm being sued."

"No, ma'am. May I come in?"

She hesitated. "Well, I don't know.... My husband tells me never to admit strangers."

"Am I a stranger? You know my name and profession."

"Nonsense. Anyone can have a card printed." But she smiled. "What is this about?"

"Your daughter Kate."

Sudden anxiety wrenched at her face. "Kate! Has... has anything happened to Kate?"

"No, ma'am. I didn't mean to frighten you. I think Kate is enjoying excellent health."

My voice and words carried more conviction than my thoughts. Because I was not at all certain about the health of Kate Wallace. She may have known what happened to Dan Varney, and if the man had been dispatched, well then....

Mrs. Lorna Wallace gulped in relief. "What about Kate?"

"I'm trying to find her."

"Is that all? Well, she lives in New York now. Works for an advertising agency. Has a wonderful job."

"She left her job," I said, "and gave up her apartment."

"What!" Mrs. Wallace goggled. She digested my words slowly and then shook her head. "Oh, but that can't be true. Kate wouldn't do a thing like that without telling me."

"How long since you've seen her?"

"About two weeks now and...." Her eyes widened. "It does seem longer than usual. Excuse me." She turned, leaving the door open, and hurried to a phone in the hallway.

I did not enter. I stayed outside, watching her make the phone call. It did not take long. She got through to Mitchell, Bodner and Olds and asked for Kate Wallace. She listened and hung up slowly, the look of disbelief on her face changing to one of dismay. She shook her head, murmuring to herself. Then she remembered and came back to the door.

"Won't you come in, Mr. Jordan."

I followed her into a small, stuffy living room. The shades were drawn to keep out the sun and the windows were closed to keep out the dust. She turned to me distractedly.

"I'm terribly concerned. I don't know what to think, Mr. Jordan. Why would she leave? And where would she go?"

"That's what I'm trying to find out."

Lorna Wallace caught a lip between her teeth. "Kate wasn't in any trouble, was she?"

"No, ma'am."

"Do you think I ought to notify the police?"

"I doubt if it would do any good."

"Why not, for heaven's sake! She disappeared, didn't she? Where else would a body go for help but the Missing Persons Bureau?"

"They'd probably tell you that Kate was not a missing person. That she left town of her own accord. There is no evidence of foul play. This is a free country, Mrs. Wallace. Kate is over twenty-one, free to go anywhere she pleases."

"But you don't understand." There was a break

in her voice and she pressed her lips together.
"Kate isn't like that. We've always been very close.
Whenever she had a problem she came to me, not
for advice, I guess, because Kate was a lot smarter
than I ever hope to be. But she would talk about it
and I'd listen and that always seemed to help. She
told me everything."

"Everything, Mrs. Wallace?"

"Yes."

"Did she ever tell you about a man named
Varney—Dan Varney?"

"Varney?" She looked blank.

"A very close friend of Kate's."

"No-o. I don't think she did." Suddenly Mrs. Wallace brightened. "A close friend, you say. Maybe he
knows where Kate went. Why don't we ask him?"

"We can't, Mrs. Wallace."

"Why not, for heaven's sake!"

"He's missing, too."

She stared for a moment, then she colored un-
comfortably. "Oh, my! You don't think they. . . ."
It was an unpleasant thought and she couldn't bear
to put it into words.

"Went away together?" I finished. "Yes, Mrs.
Wallace, I think it's not only possible but proba-
ble."

Her fingers were clasped. After a moment she
said in a low voice, "Why are you looking for my
daughter, Mr. Jordan?"

"Because I think she'll lead me to Varney. He's
the person I really want."

"Could you. . . tell me something about this man?
Is he a nice person?"

"Not especially. I think you're an intelligent

woman, Mrs. Wallace, and I'm going to be frank with you. Dan Varney left town with a lot of money that didn't belong to him."

Instantly her chin came up. There was a flash of spirit in her eyes.

"Just a moment. I know my Kate. I know her better than anyone in this whole world. We gave her a good home, Mr. Jordan, a religious home. We took her to church every Sunday. We gave her security and love. We made sacrifices and sent her to college. I watched that girl grow and develop. She never had a wrong thought or did a bad thing in her whole life. She would never get involved with an evil man. She couldn't . . . she . . . ."

Her voice faltered and her eyes swam in moisture.

"Your daughter fell in love, Mrs. Wallace," I said gently. "Varney is a very attractive and a very persuasive type. She simply could not help herself. Strong emotions sometimes obscure a person's good sense. That's what happened to Kate. She was carried away."

Mrs. Wallace had found a handkerchief. She was dabbing at her eyes. After a moment she found her voice. "I still don't understand. It just isn't like Kate to go away and not let me know. Why, she . . . she didn't even phone or write . . . or anything."

"The picture isn't all black, Mrs. Wallace."

She looked up hopefully. "What do you mean?"

"Well, for one thing, Kate is alive and, I presume, relatively happy. For another, she herself is not guilty of any crime. She had nothing to do with Varney's embezzlement and probably knows nothing about it. So it could be a lot worse. I think she left suddenly and with considerable emotional excitement. I wouldn't be at all surprised if you heard from her in the very near future.''

"You really think so?''

":I'm sure of it. When the excitement wears off, when the novelty fades, she'll suddenly realize how thoughtless and inconsiderate it was to make you worry. One of these days you'll get a wire or a long-distance phone call.''

A beaming smile wreathed her face. "Wouldn't that be wonderful?''

"I'd stake my life on it. There's one thing though, Mrs. Wallace. I'd like you to do me a favor.''

"What?''

"If Kate does call or write, would you notify me?'' She hesitated, looking dubious.

"It's for Kate's own good,'' I said. "You don't want her to get involved more deeply with Varney than necessary. Sooner or later he's going to be caught and sent away. It would be better for Kate to end this relationship at the earliest possible moment.''

She wavered, painfully deliberating. "I—I don't want to hurt Kate.''

"You'd be doing her a favor. She's in a daze, not capable of making the proper decisions. In the years to come she'll thank you a hundred times, believe me.''

Lorna Wallace stared at me uncertainly. Then, with a sudden air of resolution, she said, "Yes... yes...I'm sure you're right. If I hear from Kate, Mr. Jordan, I'll let you know.''

The drive back was uneventful. But when I reached the office I found a very peculiar state of affairs.

12

CASSIDY WAS NOT behind her desk. The telephone was ringing, but when I got to it the line was dead. The typewriter was uncovered and held a half-completed contract. It did not occur to me at the moment that anything was amiss.

The afternoon mail had been delivered and I took it into my own office. I shuffled through the envelopes and found a card from Oliver Wendell Rogers postmarked Portugal. "Retirement has its advantages, my boy. Next stop—Spain."

I smiled and put it with a pile of others I had received from various parts of Europe. They constituted a pictorial record of his round-the-world jaunt. Now in his seventies, the old boy was taking a leisurely trip, concentrating on the quirks and oddities of courtroom procedure in various countries.

I was halfway through the rest of the mail when I suddenly sat erect, acutely aware of a false note in the air. At first the trouble eluded me. And then I knew. It was the lack of sound, complete silence from out front.

I got up and crossed over to the anteroom. Still no sign of Cassidy. I knocked on the door of the washroom. No response. I called her name. Silence. I tried the door. It opened, but the room was empty.

Here was a unique experience. And very disquieting. I knew my secretary. Cassidy had a highly developed sense of duty. She was diligent and conscientious, and nothing short of a direct hit from an ICBM or orders from the Civil Defense authorities could persuade Cassidy to leave her post during office hours.

I looked for a message. Nothing. Perhaps she'd been taken ill. I felt a sharp stab of worry and reached for the telephone. I called her apartment and heard the unheeded buzz. I shook my head, baffled. Where the devil could she be?

I went back to my office and tried to work. But it was no use. I couldn't concentrate. I decided to call hospitals. I got out the classified directory and was turning pages when the door opened and there she was.

Cassidy, one hundred and fifty pounds of bristling female. Fists on hips, lips tightened to a thin line, she stood and glowered darkly. Even so, in her black and formidable mood, she looked better to me at the moment than a Balinese dancing girl with wanton eyes and a promising smile.

"Well?" she demanded in a highly indignant tone.

"Well what?" I asked.

"Why the runaround?"

"I don't know what you're talking about. And stop glaring at me. I'm the aggrieved party, not you. I come back to the office and find it deserted. Nobody here to receive papers or clients or phone calls. You leave the door open and the petty cash unguarded, and then you come barging in sore as a boil. Now I don't mind an occasional coffee break, but when—"

It was too much for Cassidy. Outraged color flooded her face. "Coffee break!" she exploded, and for a moment was utterly incapable of speech.

I grinned. "Simmer down. I was only kidding."

She found her tongue. "Some joke. Ha, ha!"

"Where have you been?"

"The police station."

"What!"

"That's right. Tenth Precinct."

"Why?"

"Because I thought you sent for me." Her temperature was cooling perceptibly.

"Now, wait a minute," I said. "Let's take it slow and from the beginning. Come over here and sit down. Good. Now tell me exactly what happened."

Cassidy drew a breath. "I was typing the Empire Realty contracts about an hour ago when the telephone rang. It was a man. He told me he was Lieutenant Madigan and that you were in trouble. He said you drove through a traffic signal and hit a pedestrian and the man was seriously injured. They were holding you on charges and that you wanted me to come down for urgent instructions."

I looked at her blankly, at a loss. "What happened?"

"Of course I left immediately. But there wasn't any Lieutenant Madigan at the station house. I asked the desk sergeant if they were holding a lawyer named Scott Jordan and he said no. He thought maybe I had the wrong precinct, but the man on the phone had given me the address, so I knew I hadn't made a mistake. The whole thing was a false alarm. I came back to the office.''

"Strange," I said thoughtfully.

"No accident, Scott?"

"No. The call was a fake."

"But why?"

"I don't know."

"Somebody's idea of a practical joke?"

"I doubt it."

But an idea was digesting in my head. I thought of Sergeant Ernie Strobe. He knew I had an affidavit from Fred Duncan. He hoped perhaps to filch it from the files, and then had to cancel his plans when something went wrong. The idea lacked protein. What if he did get the affidavit? What would he accomplish? I could always draw a new one.

Unless, of course, something happened to Fred Duncan.

I sought other explanations but failed to strike a spark. In the meantime Cassidy was checking the office. She came back to report that everything seemed intact, including the petty cash. I sat back, irritated by a nagging curiosity.

Strobe was the principal irritant. His image kept reappearing. It finally suggested my next move.

"I'm going to the library," I told Cassidy. "Lock up at five-thirty."

It was almost that now. Buildings were already disgorging workers, heads bent and moving toward subway kiosks. Traffic clogged the streets, an unmoving, honking mass coughing exhaust fumes. I walked south.

The two stone lions flanking the public library kept an impassive vigil on the parade. I passed between them and entered the building. There was a musty odor in the room containing old newspaper files.

I checked the index and wrote out a slip for *The New York Times.* What I wanted were back copies covering the story of Ben Keller's exit from the Crescent Hotel.

They came on microfilm and I settled back to make notes. How, I wondered, would Sergeant Ernie Strobe react if he could see me now? Exhuming details.

If was front-page news, even in the staid and venerable *Times.* There was a picture of Strobe, emerging from a departmental investigation, his face stony and expressionless. And a picture of the District Attorney, too, delivering an irate statement castigating the whole detail. Negligence, they said. Nobody openly accusing Strobe or his men of complicity.

I copied a list of the men on duty with Strobe that night. There might be one among them who would support Duncan's story. And others, no doubt, who wanted it suppressed. The passage of time had given them a feeling of security. Had Strobe alerted them now to a threatened danger? Were they being mobilized to present a united front? One thing was sure. Among this coterie, Duncan's book would induce some jittery and sleepless nights.

There was a telephone booth on the main floor. I patronized it and called Max Turner.

"No news," he reported. "That Varney must have fallen through a hole in the earth. I've got three men working on it and not a smell."

"Keep trying," I said. "In the meantime I have another chore. Have you got a pencil handy?"

"Yes. Shoot."

"Here's a list of names." I sketched the facts briefly. "I want some background material on them. A few may have retired. Others may still be on the force. Find out where they're assigned and how they're fixed financially."

"We're running up a bill here, Counselor."

"I'll send you a check tomorrow."

"We may need a few more men."

"Use your own judgment, Max. Whatever is necessary to get results."

He promised to start at once and we hung up.

13

I DID NOT SEE ANY of the Colemans over the weekend. On Monday morning, shortly after ten, I had a pair of visitors at the office. Cassidy brought me a neatly engraved card that said: Bradford Cornell, Attorney- at-Law.

"He's not alone," she said.

"Who's with him?"

"A lady. Mrs. M. Parker Coleman."

I gave an involuntary start of surprise. "Well, well," I murmured. "The widow. Lorraine Coleman. Show them in, by all means."

I was standing when they entered. The lawyer was an elderly gent, tall and silver-haired and distinguished. I scarcely noticed him. He was totally eclipsed by the woman.

In our society we breed a certain type of female who is seldom plagued by the economic facts of life. She possesses qualities relentlessly and unremittingly in demand. Chalk it up to male hormones, the drive to propagate, to conquer, whatever. There is always some ardent male panting at her heels, avid for scraps, eager to pick up the tab regardless of cost. You can see her in many places, on Fifth Avenue draped in mink, on the Riviera behind sunglasses, on the fantail of a yacht in a bikini, but

never—absolutely never—behind the counter of a
store, in front of a typewriter, or toiling at any
other mundane task. She belongs, with her assets
and attractions, to a special privileged class, the
sorority of beautiful and desirable women.

My own pulse stayed normal. But then old M.P.
had different standards and different tastes. I could
understand his bewitchment, since I was not blind,
and why he had coveted this particular item. When
she raised her veil I saw a pale, luminous com-
plexion, restless eyes, and a passionate, discon-
tented mouth. Her hair was raven-wing black and
silky.

"May I offer my condolences," I said.

She dipped her chin one millimeter in acknowl-
edgment.

I waved to a pair of chairs and they sat. I sat, too,
and looked at them across the desk expectantly.
Bradford Cornell cleared his throat with a sonorous
rumble.

"Mrs. Coleman," he said, "has retained me to
probate her husband's estate."

Bully for you, I thought. The estate was worth
some four million dollars, which meant a sizable
fee. But I did not congratulate him aloud. I sat and
waited politely for him to continue.

He smiled. Excellent dentures glistened in the
morning sunlight. "We have a bit of a problem, Mr.
Jordan. Perhaps you can help us."

"In what way?" I wondered if he knew I was
Adam's lawyer.

"Mr. Coleman executed his will some years ago,
shortly after his second marriage. His lawyer, as
you probably know, was Oliver Wendell Rogers."

"Yes. I worked for Mr. Rogers at the time."

"Were you, perhaps, one of the attesting witnesses?"

"I was, together with my secretary, who also worked for Rogers."

The lawyer and his client exchanged deadpan glances.

"Are you by any chance acquainted with the contents of that will?" Cornell inquired.

"No, sir, I merely attested Mr. Coleman's signature."

"But a copy was available in the files if you wanted to look at it."

"I suppose so."

"You never tried?"

I shook my head. I had no idea what they wanted and his oblique approach was beginning to annoy me. "It was none of my business," I said. "I am not a nosy individual."

"No offense intended," he said in quick apology. He coughed politely. "Do you remember what Mr. Rogers did with the will after it was signed?"

"That was a good many years ago. He probably gave the original to Mr. Coleman and filed the copy."

"And when, if I may inquire, did Mr. Rogers retire from the practice of law?"

"About seven years ago."

"Is it true that he turned his practice over to you?"

"It's true up to a point. Certainly you realize that the services rendered by a lawyer are highly personal. Some of Mr. Rogers's clients stayed with me, others moved elsewhere. M. Parker Coleman was one of them."

"But most of the files were left in your care."

"Yes."

"I assume that would include a copy of Mr. Coleman's will."

"Probably."

He sat back, trying to look casual and unconcerned. "I wonder if you'd let us see it."

"Well, now...." I lifted an eyebrow and glanced at Lorraine Coleman. She had bent forward, her eyes dark and intent. "Isn't that a rather unusual request?" I said.

"Not at all." She spoke for the first time. Her tone was austere and brusque. "I'm his widow. I have a right to see the contents of his will."

"You do indeed. And I'm sure the original is available to you. Why don't you look for it in Mr. Coleman's safe-deposit box?"

"How we go about it is none of your affair."

Cornell's hands fluttered at the widow in a placating gesture. "Please, Mrs. Coleman. Let me handle this." He returned to me with an awkward smile. "The fact is, Mr. Jordan, we visited the bank on Friday. He had a box at the Merchant's Trust and we opened it pursuant to an order signed by the surrogate for just that purpose, to find a will."

"And?"

"Well, sir, the box contained stocks, bonds, deeds, all manner of documents." He gestured eloquently. "But no will."

"Have you looked elsewhere?"

"Yes. We spent the entire weekend searching.

We went through his papers at home, all of them, without success."

"Perhaps he destroyed it."

My words were a catalytic agent. They got an abrupt and violent reaction. Lorraine Coleman surged to her feet, blazing. Her head strained back, neck muscles taut. *"Never!"* Her voice quivered with venom. "How dare you suggest such a thing!"

Cornell went to her at once. "Please, Mrs. Coleman." He spoke to her cajolingly and patted her arms and finally got her to sit down. But the volcano was still seething. I could see it in her eyes and in the tight compression of her lips, white with wrath.

I knew what ailed the widow.

Somebody had explained the law to her.

It was quite simple. If a man destroys his will, then he dies intestate, and the statutes control distribution of his property. The statutes are clear and precise on the subject.

No will: one-third goes to the widow and two-thirds go to the decedent's children.

Lorraine Coleman had expected to inherit the whole four million dollars. Without a will she would lose something under three million. That hurt. It hurt badly. But what hurt even more was the thought of sharing the estate with Adam and Barbara and Victoria. The prospect was anathema. No wonder she was so vehement.

Bradford Cornell faced my desk and spread his hands apologetically. "Forgive her, Mr. Jordan. She's quite distressed at this development."

"Naturally."

He either missed or ignored the irony in my tone. "We'd like you to cooperate."

"How?"

"If a copy of the will is available I'd like to file it in court."

I sat and considered his request. It placed me in a peculiar position. Under certain circumstances the carbon copy of a will may be admitted to probate. This would leave my people out in the cold.

Here was a reprieve for Adam. The opportunity to inherit a fortune and preserve his fiscal neck.

And yet, both morally and legally, I had no right to withhold or suppress a copy of the will. The widow was entitled to it and a court order could force me to produce it.

I touched the buzzer and when Cassidy appeared I said, "Would you check the files, please, and see if there's a folder on M. Parker Coleman. I'd like the copy of his last will and testament."

She nodded and closed the door.

Dialogue was suspended while we waited. The silence was palpable. Lorraine Coleman sat tensely forward. Bradford Cornell stood behind her, hands resting lightly and reassuringly on her shoulders. Muted traffic noises floated up from the street. Cassidy seemed to be taking a long time, so I excused myself and went out front.

Several drawers were open and she was riffling through them. "What's the trouble?" I asked.

"Can't seem to find it," she said. "Nothing on M. Parker Coleman at all. Not here, nor in the dead files either."

"Are you sure?"

"Positive."

"I seem to recollect that we once had a folder on the old boy."

"I thought so, too. But it's been a long time since I had occasion to look for it."

"Perhaps we forwarded everything to his new attorneys after Rogers retired."

She moved her shoulders. "I just don't remember."

I went back and rejoined the pair in my office. Lorraine Coleman glanced up eagerly. I spread my hands and made the announcement.

"Sorry. We have no papers on your husband at all."

For a moment she looked stunned. Under the translucent skin drained of color, her cheekbones stood out. She began to tremble. She rose suddenly, pulling violently free of Cornell's steadying hands.

"Do you think you can get away with this? I know what you're trying to do, you...you shyster." Her voice was thick and strangled. "I'll have you disbarred if it takes every cent I own. I—"

Cornell got a grip on her shoulders again, trying to dam the flow. "Mrs. Coleman, please—"

She swung on him, raging. "I knew it. I warned you. I told you it would be futile to come here. This man is Adam's lawyer. He wants Adam to inherit. He's hidden the copy or destroyed it. He's a disgrace to the legal profession. A cheap, chiseling shyster. I'm going to report him to the Bar Association. I want everyone to know what kind of...."

Cornell towered over her. He pushed at the air with both hands, his resonant baritone rising about the tirade. "Now, Mrs. Coleman...now, Mrs.

Coleman...control yourself. We'll never accomplish anything with irresponsible accusations—"

"Irresponsible!" Her voice quivered with indignation. She concentrated the blue glare on her lawyer. "Whose side are you on, anyway?"

"Yours, of course. But—"

"Let her rant," I said calmly. "Get the poison out of her system."

But I was wrong. The outburst had no therapeutic effect. With three million dollars at stake her rancor fed itself. She swung back to me, shaking with impotent fury. But I got no more invective. The vitriol had clogged her throat and I saw the muscles in it working spasmodically.

Cornell tried to apologize. "I'm sorry, Counselor. She's not herself. Her husband's illness, his death, the loss of the will...she's not responsible. Please forgive her."

I shrugged, then turned and walked to the window. I could see their reflection as he steered her firmly toward the door. And I expelled a sigh of relief when he got her out. But the relief did not last. Almost immediately I heard a commotion in the outer office. I heard Cassidy's voice and I reached the door in a single lunge.

Mrs. Coleman had balked on the way out. She wanted Cornell to make an independent search of the files. Apparently he had objected and so she had started for the files herself.

I cannot remember laying forceful hands on a female except once in my life, three years ago, and that was to save my hide when a lady with an illogical grievance came at me with a loaded .22. My sole interest at that time was to disarm her. But if

Lorraine Coleman so much as yanked at a single drawer of my files I had every intention of tossing her out into the hall on her very shapely posterior.

Cassidy saved me the trouble.

She had moved with surprising speed, arms folded, planting herself in front of the cabinets like Horatius defending the bridge. She made a formidable figure. And even Lorraine, wrought up and desperate, thought twice before attempting to dislodge her.

Once again, Cornell filled the breach. He got another grip on the lady's arm and nudged her through the door. I walked over and closed it behind them.

"Well!" Cassidy exclaimed. "What was that all about?"

"She thinks we're lying. She says we have a copy of the will and we're suppressing it."

"Why would we do that?"

"To benefit Adam and the rest of Coleman's progeny." I looked at her thoughtfully. "Can you recall any attempt by Coleman to revoke his will?"

She considered it. "He may have had a change of heart. People are always destroying old wills and writing new ones. If he did, he called Mr. Rogers and told him he was tearing up his will and please destroy the copy. I wouldn't know. Mr. Rogers didn't tell me everything."

"But you do remember the contents of the will?"

"Well enough. After all, I typed the document. I remember he left everything to his wife and I remember Mr. Rogers arguing with him, protesting that it was unfair to his children."

I nodded and went back to my office. I thought of

Lorraine Coleman, consumed by greed. No matter what happened, whether a will was found or not, she would inherit over a million dollars. Wasn't that enough for her? Or did she feel she had earned more? So much for each year of her life squandered on a man twice her age with a stalling motor in his chest.

14

BARBARA WAS BACK AT WORK. She had engaged a telephone-answering service and the girl gave me a number where she could be reached. She was at some photographic studio and when I got through to her she could only spare a moment, so I came straight to the point.

"Dinner tonight?"

"Well, I. . . ." She hesitated.

"Some quiet place."

"All right, Scott."

"Pick you up at seven."

There was a note on my desk reminding me to send a check to Max Turner. I tore a blank from the book and was filling it in when Cassidy appeared at the door with a blue-backed legal document.

"Just served on us," she said, "by a clerk from Irving Birnbaum's office."

It was a motion for summary judgment in the case of *Fred Duncan* v. *Adam Coleman*, returnable five days hence in Special Term, Part I of the Supreme Court. The attached affidavit claimed that our defense was sham, frivolous, and without merit, interposed merely to delay the proceedings. And of course, Birnbaum was right. He was also, as I had anticipated, on his toes.

"What now?" Cassidy asked.

"We don't have much choice. We'll contest the motion and see what happens."

"Don't you know?"

"Yes," I said sourly. "The motion will probably be granted. Nevertheless, get your notebook and I'll dictate an answer."

In the meantime I called Max.

"Just going to phone you, Counselor," he said. "About that list of cops you gave me."

I sat erect. "Yes. I'm listening."

"I spoke to one of them myself. A man named Gus Suchak. He got abusive and warned me to lay off. Since then he's had a couple of meetings with Strobe."

"Gus Suchak, eh?"

"That's right. Not only was he a member of the detail guarding Ben Keller that night, but he was on duty at the time Keller took his dive."

"Keep digging, Max. I have a check for you. Do you want to pick it up or shall I mail it?"

"Mail it," he said.

Cassidy had returned with her steno pad. I dictated, trying to improvise a valid defense where one did not really exist. It involved some agile semantics, but I doubted if the judge would be taken in.

"You have a real-estate closing with Buchwald at two-thirty," she reminded me. "I have the papers ready for you."

"That means I'll be tied up for the rest of the afternoon."

"Then you won't be back."

"No. I have a dinner appointment at seven."

When I reached Barbara's apartment I was surprised to find the whole clan gathered there,
waiting for me. Victoria Dodd looked severe in
mourning black. Gil Dodd sat beside her, his square
brown face sober and thoughtful. Adam was
prowling the room and he moved toward me, his
eyes intense under a striated brow.

"I had a call from Lorraine's lawyer, Scott. Chap
named Bradford Cornell. He said they were having
trouble locating dad's will, and did I have any
suggestions. I told him no. Then his voice changed.
It suddenly grew sharp and tough. He said you
had a copy in your office, but you were suppressing it, probably at my request and for my benefit.
He said he intended to learn the truth and take
measures."

"What kind of measures?"

"A criminal prosecution against us if necessary."

"On what grounds?"

"Conspiracy to defraud. I could hear Lorraine's
voice in the background, railing at him and egging
him on. She sounded half-hysterical."

"I know. They were in my office this morning."

"Cornell advised me to reconsider. You know
what I did? I hung up on him."

"Rude," I said. "But effective."

"Anyway, I thought the family ought to discuss it with you. When I called Barbara she told
me you'd be here this evening. So I got in touch
with Vickie and Gil and asked them to meet us
here."

"What does it mean?" Barbara asked.

"Just what you heard," I said. "Cornell can't

find the original will and I can't find the copy. Naturally, your stepmother is frantic.''

''But why?''

''Because now your father's estate may be distributed according to the rules of intestacy.''

She looked at me helplessly.

Gil Dodd supplied the definition. ''Intestacy prevails when a man leaves no will.''

''Instead of being disinherited completely,'' I said, ''with the whole estate going to Lorraine, she would get only a third, and the rest would go to you and Adam and Victoria, to be divided three ways.''

They were staring at me.

''Unless,'' I added, ''the will is found.''

''It won't be,'' Victoria announced firmly. ''Of course dad had a change of heart. He realized how wrong it was, how utterly unjust to disinherit his own children and leave everything to that dreadful woman.''

A thin smile touched Barbara's mouth. ''Ironic, isn't it? Lorraine married dad for his money. Take the lion's share away and it negates all those years she forced herself to spend with him.''

''Let me get this straight,'' Adam said. ''There must have been a copy of the will. Don't lawyers generally keep a carbon in the files?''

''That is the usual procedure.''

''And didn't Rogers leave his files in your custody when he retired?''

''He did.''

''Well, what happened to it?''

''I don't know.''

''How about Rogers? Wouldn't he know?''

''Mr. Rogers is traveling in Europe and I don't

know where to reach him. There is one thing, however, I'd like to make absolutely clear." I paused and took them all in with my eyes. "I am not your benefactor. I have not suppressed the copy of your father's will in order to put money in anybody's pocket. I admit the sum is temptingly large, but something even larger is involved, a matter of ethics and my position as a lawyer."

Gil Dodd smiled. "Nobody suggested otherwise."

"Lorraine suggests otherwise."

Adam was frowning. "Are you telling us, Scott, that a missing will cannot be probated?"

"No such thing. The surrogate may probate a lost or missing will if its provisions can be clearly and distinctly proved."

"How can they if the will is missing?"

"By the testimony of at least two credible witnesses. And the court will accept a correct copy as equivalent to one of the witnesses."

"Then Lorraine may freeze us out after all."

"The possibility exists. But she would first have to prove that the will was in existence at the time of your father's death or was fraudulently destroyed during his lifetime."

"Can she do that?"

"She'll certainly try."

"By God, we'll fight her all the way!"

"I think you should."

Adam glanced at Victoria and got a vigorous nod. He turned to Barbara and got another nod. He came back to me.

"All right, Scott. We're agreed. We'd like you to represent us in this matter. If there's going to be a legal fight over the estate, you're the man to handle it."

"You understand," I told them, "that a will contest can be long and costly."

"Yes." Victoria nodded. "And we feel you should have a retainer. Adam is hard-pressed at the moment, so Gil has generously offered to advance the money." She looked at him. "Gil."

He withdrew a checkbook from his breast pocket and spread it open on my desk. "Will five hundred cover it?" he asked.

"Now, Gil," his wife said. "We agreed on a thousand. Let's not quibble."

Dodd exhaled a sigh and began writing in the neat precise hand of an accountant. The family dispute that cut his wife out of her father's will had also cost him his job. Gil Dodd, I recalled, had been an auditor in one of the Coleman Hotels when he first met the boss's daughter. Victoria was no beauty, but she did represent a large step up the ladder. His courtship encountered no obstacles. Victoria needed a husband and Mr. Parker Coleman was pleased to assist. Dodd was, after all, a professional man, a C.P.A. with a record of competence and efficiency.

Old M.P. had footed the bill for a splashy wedding and within a year his new son-in-law became chief auditor for the entire Coleman chain. Dodd's ability and diligence quickly stifled any indictment for nepotism. But it didn't last. Dodd got axed when the old man disinherited his brood. He was in private practice now and doing fairly well.

Adam watched him with a frown of embarrassment. "Thanks, Gil. This is a temporary loan, you know."

Dodd shrugged. It was money down the drain if Adam lost his inheritance. And if he lost the Duncan case, too, Adam would be in hock up to his ears.

"Then it's settled," Victoria said. She leaned over and pecked at Barbara's cheek. "We're going back to the apartment, Adam. Come back with us."

He nodded and we shook hands all around.

When they were gone, Barbara said, "I don't much feel like going out. Why don't we take pot-luck here?"

"Too much trouble."

"I don't mind."

I did not expect much, so of course it came as a surprise. I got my first inkling when I sniffed the air, a savory and redolent odor emanating from the kitchen. And the product, veal fricassee, lived up to its advance billing. Her coffee, too, was no synthetic brew from an instant-type jar.

I lost momentum over the third cup. "You have unsuspected talents."

"Some people paint. My creative outlet is cooking."

"In your hands, undoubtedly an art form."

"Thank you." She leaned her chin on a closed hand. "Adam tells me you hired a private detective to find Dan. Any luck?"

"Not yet. Did he ever express any preferences about travel? Hawaii? Switzerland?"

"Not Switzerland. Dan liked warm climates."

New York, I thought, would be warm enough, if

we ever got him back here. And the temperature would rise in direct proportion to the amount of money he had spent. Fred Duncan would stoke the furnace and the District Attorney would open the flue.

"And what about Kate Wallace, Scott?"

"No trace of her, either."

Barbara shook her head. "They talk about women's intuition. Look how frequently we go wrong."

"There's a blind spot where men are concerned."

"But why? What makes us so susceptible?"

"Human fallibility. The need to be loved. Fear of being alone. Any number of things."

"And you, Scott? Are you immune?"

"We're talking about women."

"Is there any essential difference?"

"Well, now . . . ."

"I mean emotionally."

"Yes. Women play a different role in life. Child-bearing for example. Their emotional requirements are different."

"Perhaps. Have you never been captivated by the wrong woman?"

"Several times. Chalk it up to nagging hormones."

"I'm glad to hear you have them."

"Did you doubt it?"

"Yes."

"Why, for Pete's sake!"

She looked at me with her head tilted to one side. "Do you consider me attractive?"

"An arthritic octogenarian would turn handsprings for one of your smiles."

"But not you?"

"What does that mean?"

"Scott, you're the first man I ever met who never even tried to make a pass at me."

"I didn't want to imitate the herd."

"Some things in life are universal, boy, and you don't have to be different."

There is a time for words and a time for action.

She had looks, intelligence, and a gustatory flair—the situation was fraught with peril.

Tonight I felt reckless.

15

As an appurtenance of modern civilization the telephone is unquestionably indispensable. It is also the source of limitless irritations. Chief among them is the ringing device which can and does trespass on a man's privacy regardless of the hour.

It was three o'clock on Tuesday morning when it woke me out of a sound sleep. For a moment I was tempted to muffle the instrument. But I swallowed the impulse. It might be an emergency. Crime, like illness, strikes at odd hours. A lawyer, like a doctor, should be available when needed. I fumbled in the darkness, got the handset, and mumbled incoherently.

"Scott!" Adam's voice was feverish and taut as a piano string.

Its urgency brought me fully awake on the instant. "Yes. What is it?"

"I'm in trouble. Can you come at once?"

"Where are you?"

"The Tenth Precinct. It's on—"

"I know where it is. Sit tight."

I hopped out of bed, splashed cold water at my face, and slid into a suit. Downstairs, I flagged a taxi. "Two-thirty Twentieth Street and step on it."

The address was a familiar one to me. It housed

the Homicide Squad and the office of Detective-lieutenant John Nola, an old friend. He was on duty when I got there and the desk sergeant sent me up.

Nola was a dark, slender man with deep-set eyes, alert, direct, and absolutely incorruptible. A career cop who, despite years on the force, still retained a quality of compassion. In the past I had represented several clients in cases under his investigation.

His attitude now was brisk and businesslike. He nodded shortly and indicated a chair.

"Where's my client?" I asked, declining the offer.

"In the squad room, still being questioned. I wanted to talk to you first."

"What's he doing?"

"He was caught transporting a dead body. He may be responsible for making the body dead."

I sat down heavily. "Who's the victim?"

"An ex-cop, Fred Duncan."

"Tell me about it, John."

He leaned his elbows on the desk, fingers clasped. "One of our radio cars was cruising along Riverside Drive at 11:15 P.M. About Seventy-eighth Street they spotted a 1975 Chevrolet proceeding north. It was slapping along on a flat tire. But at Ninety-sixth Street it failed to turn off and kept going. That made them suspicious. Why would a man deliberately ruin a good wheel and grind up a tire? So they closed in and stopped him.

"Your man Coleman was behind the wheel. He had a passenger in the front seat. When the boys flashed their light, they saw he was dead. He'd been struck three blows at the back of the skull by a heavy instrument. They found the instrument on the floor behind the front seat, a bloodstained jack handle."

"Any fingerprints?" I asked.

"Smudged."

"Where was he taking the body?"

"He refused to say."

"But he must have offered some explanation."

"Only that he'd been working late at his office, and that when he came down to his drive home he found Duncan's body in the car. He admitted that he knew the man. He also conceded there was some kind of trouble between them. After that, nothing. He clammed up and refused to talk until he'd called his lawyer."

"How did he act?"

"Dazed. Like a man who'd been drugged."

"May I see him, John?"

"Later. Let's talk first. What kind of trouble were they having?"

With Nola, I seldom played any cards close to the vest unless trial strategy called for a surprise. But the lawsuit was a matter of public record and he could find out about it easily enough. So I told him about Duncan's book, about the movie sale and about Varney's disappearance.

"Then Duncan was holding your client personally responsible for the two hundred thousand dollars."

"Yes."

"And no complaint was filed against Varney?"

"No, sir."

"Why the hell not?"

"We were trying to protect the reputation of Coleman's agency."

"So you let an embezzler go scot-free."

"Not exactly, John. I have Max Turner and a couple of men looking for him."

"Varney's a crook. Finding him is our job, not yours."

"Can you spare the men, Lieutenant? Would you send someone abroad if the clues pointed to Europe or—"

"All right," he cut in. "I see your point." He reached for the phone and issued instructions.

I was shocked when they brought Adam in. His eyes were numb and stupefied in a face drained to a sickly gray. A detective led him to a chair, and then he stood as if in a hypnotic trance.

"Sit down," Nola said.

He obeyed automatically.

I called his name sharply. *"Adam!"*

He turned, blinked, and then managed a cramped smile that dissolved instantly.

"There seems to be a misunderstanding here," I said with the false heartiness of a doctor diagnosing a thrombosis. "They tell me you were carting a dead body around town without an undertaker's license. You ought to know that's against the law, Adam. What happened?"

His eyes veered to Nola and back to me.

"You can talk," I said. "Tell us about it."

His throat worked. After a moment he took a breath and spoke. "I—I had dinner alone this evening and went back to the office. These last few days . . . so many distractions . . . I was way behind. Manuscripts piling up. I read until my eyes blurred, about eleven, I guess, then I went down to the car. A man was sitting in the front seat. I—I didn't know he was dead until I opened the door and the light went on."

"Where was the car parked?"

"On a side street between First and Second."

"All right. Go ahead."

He swallowed hugely. "A dead body in the car. I . . . well, it panicked me. I didn't know what to do. Then I got in and started driving."

"Why?"

He looked blank.

"Why did you start driving, Adam? Why didn't you call a cop?"

"I was afraid. I thought, here's Duncan, dead in my car, murdered. They'll blame me. They'll say I owed him two hundred thousand dollars. I won't have a chance. Jesus, how could I call the cops? They'd crucify me."

"Where were you taking the body?"

"I don't know. Anywhere I could get rid of it. I just kept driving."

"You knew the tire was flat?"

"Yes."

"But you didn't stop."

"How could I? If I called a mechanic, he'd spot the body. If I fixed it myself, somebody might look into the car. I was afraid to stop."

The phone rang and Nola took it. He listened briefly and hung up.

"Office of the Medical Examiner," he said. "The serologist just typed the blood on the jack handle. It matches Duncan's. So does the hair."

None of us had expected anything different. But they were building a case.

I said, "Look at me, Adam."

He lifted his face and our eyes met.

"Did you kill him?"

"No. I swear it."

"All right, then. Lieutenant Nola as going to ask you some questions. I want you to answer them fully and truthfully. If you're innocent you have nothing to hide. But if you lie, if you hold back, if you try to evade, he'll know it, believe me."

Adam nodded and faced the lieutenant.

Nola leaned forward. "Had you seen Duncan earlier today or spoken to him?"

"No, sir."

"Had you made a previous appointment with him?"

"No, sir."

"About the proceeds of that movie sale—Duncan clearly understood it was your partner Varney who stole the money."

"Jordan explained it to him."

"Yet he was holding you personally responsible."

"Yes, sir."

Nola regarded him musingly. "We know a few things about Duncan. First he had an invalid wife to support. Then some hophead with a gun crippled him. His wife died and his only son was killed by a hit-and-run driver. He's trying to help support a daughter-in-law and two kids. The loss of that money must have been a bitter blow. We also know that he had a temper."

Adam said nothing.

"Had he ever threatened you?"

"With physical violence?"

"Yes."

"Once. But I don't think he meant it."

"Let's get back to your car. It's a 1975 model."

"Yes, sir."

"With only nine thousand miles on it."

"I don't use it very much."

"Any trouble with the tires lately?"

I saw his point and broke in impulsively. "Of course. Whoever killed Duncan let the air out of that tire to make sure Adam couldn't drive away. Insurance that he'd be caught. We can prove that by showing there isn't any leak."

Adam had perked up. Nola's words deflated him.

"There is now. Driving any distance on a flat tire cuts it to ribbons."

I nodded glumly. "Maybe we can't prove it. But my theory still remains valid."

"As theory only."

"How long was Duncan dead when you found him?"

"An hour—two at most. Rigor had not set in."

The door opened and a detective poked his head through. "Magowan's here, Lieutenant."

"Ed Magowan?" I asked.

"Yes, sir. He wants to question the suspect."

"All right," Nola said. "Let him do it in the squad room. I'm through with him for the time being."

Adam turned his worry-kneaded face to me.

"It's routine," I told him. "Magowan's from the D.A.'s office. They like to keep a man on top of every homicide case from the beginning. Just stick to your story. Answer his questions, but don't volunteer any information."

"Will you wait for me?"

"It won't do any good," Nola said evenly. "We'll have to keep you in custody."

Apparently, Adam didn't quite realize his predicament. "On what grounds?"

"Suspicion of homicide."

16

"I KNOW MY CLIENT," I told Nola when we were alone. "He's not the type for violence."

"There is no type," Nola said. "It happens time and again. First an argument, noises in the throat followed by adrenalin in the blood. Then blind anger. Coleman is desperate. Duncan is an embittered hothead. They meet and the sparks fly. Coleman may or may not have been prepared, but the jack handle is within reach. He wields it and then twice more just to make sure. A moment of unreasoning insanity and then he realizes what he'd done."

"I won't buy it, John."

Nola shrugged. Smoke from one of his thin, dappled cigars curled past his brooding eyes. Had Nola been more of a politician, had he been able to exercise more tact, he might now be ensconced in a high administrative post. Though I doubted that he even wanted such a job. He preferred to be a working cop.

"Does that mean you're convinced?" I asked him.

"It means we can make out a pretty good case right now. We can prove means, motive and opportunity."

"But you can't wrap it up at this stage," I said.

"Perhaps not. Can you name me another candidate, Counselor?"

"Yes. One of the men in the department."

"What department?"

"The Police Department."

His flat stomach crowded against the desk. "Say that again, please."

"You want another candidate? I say there's one right here in the Police Department."

"Boil it down, Counselor. Who?"

"Sergeant Ernie Strobe."

Nola ground out his cigar. He looked me up and down with long-faced deliberation. "Do you have any evidence?"

"Not a shred. You didn't ask for proof. You asked for a candidate and I'm nominating one."

"Why Strobe?"

"Do you know the man?"

"I know him," the lieutenant said in a flat voice. "What's the connection?"

"Remember the Jaekel-Keller case?"

"You mean when our star witness fell out of a window."

I lifted an eyebrow. "*Fell?*"

"Italicize the word if you like, Counselor. However it happened, Ben Keller got himself dead and the prosecution collapsed. I assume you have a point to make. Let's have it."

"Do you recall the name of the man who was supposed to be guarding Keller that night?"

"Yes. Ernie Strobe."

"And the name of the men working that detail with him?"

His brow furrowed. "Refresh my recollection."

Silence for a moment. "I'm still listening, Counselor."

"The book Fred Duncan wrote, the one my client sold to the movies, was a fictionalized version of what really happened that night at the Crescent Hotel. According to Duncan, there was a payoff. Two of Jaekel's torpedoes were passed into Keller's room. The witness had to be silenced. When he refused to cooperate, they helped him over the sill."

The lieutenant's narrow face hardened into a set expression. "Strobe's palm was greased?"

"So Duncan claimed."

"And Strobe knew about the book?"

"He not only knew about it, he threatened an injunction against the movie company."

"But the book was already sold. What could he gain by Duncan's death?"

"Plenty. If he sued the film company, they would need Duncan's testimony. With Duncan dead, they might think twice about shooting the picture after all."

"Have you spoken to Strobe?"

"Yes. I was in Coleman's office when he stormed in and demanded to see a copy of the manuscript."

Nola slapped his palms on the desk. His face was a carving in stone. He said grittily, "Keller's death left a stench in the department. It tainted every cop on the force with the stigma of corruption. I felt it in my guts and asked to be assigned to the case. But they turned me down. It was out of my jurisdiction, they said. We couldn't step on anybody's toes."

"What were they afraid of?"

"The truth, maybe. How would it look if we proved bribery, corruption, obstruction of justice in the very agency charged with law enforcement? It was an election year and the orders came from City Hall. They were afraid of political repercussions."

"Could they muzzle the District Attorney, too?"

"Indirectly. By not cooperating."

"So Keller's death was fobbed off as a suicide."

"That's what they sold to the public. Or tried to, anyway. Keller, they said, had been frightened and was brooding. Threats had been made against his family. The man lacked stamina. He lacked moral fiber. He was incapable of facing up to a trial and the ultimate vengeance of Jaekel's organization."

But the public, I remembered, had been skeptical. And, as usual, apathetic—passive in its complacency. The initial sense of outrage had gradually cooled under a cloak of self-deception.

Nola kicked his chair back and stood up. "Let's have a talk with Ernie Strobe right now."

"At this hour?"

"Why not?"

Why not, indeed, I thought. Something might slip out before the sergeant could clear the cobwebs from a sleep-drugged brain.

IT WAS A MODEST, middle-income neighborhood. If Strobe had an additional source of revenue, he was sage enough not to let it show while he was still on the force. And he slept like a man with a clear conscience.

It took five minutes to rouse him out of bed. He answered the door, rumpled and puffy-eyed. But when he recognized his visitors he came sharply and watchfully awake.

"Lieutenant Nola!"

"I have some questions, Strobe. Open up."

He stepped aside. I followed Nola into the living room. No mass-produced, overstuffed, cut-rate items here. These furnishings would fit nicely into classier quarters when he finally retired. Strobe excused himself, went into the next room and came back shrugging into a terry-cloth robe. His eyes spared me a brief glance and came to rest on the lieutenant.

"Been sleeping long?" Nola asked him.

"Since about midnight. I got in about eleven."

"When did you go off duty?"

"Yesterday, at five o'clock. Today was my day off." His mouth tightened. "I seem to be on the grill for something, Lieutenant. Why? What's all this sudden interest in my activities?"

"We'll get to that in a moment, Strobe. Just answer my questions."

"No, sir. With all due respect to your rank, Lieutenant. I'm on the Rackets Squad, not under your command. You happen to be in my apartment. It's four-thirty in the morning. I have a right to know what you're after."

Nola stared at him frostily. His voice was abrasive. "You're a police officer, Strobe. Although I have some personal opinions on the subject." He paused to let the comment sink in. "You know my job. You know I'm attached to Homicide. I'm here because a murder has been committed and it's my job to find the murderer. To do that I have to ask questions. So I'm starting with you, Strobe, and sure as you're standing on God's green footstool you're going to answer everything I put to you—with deference if not with candor. Balk and I'll have you hauled over the coals on departmental charges. If you think that's an idle threat, test me."

Strobe kept himself under white-faced control. But I saw a vein bulge in a blue diagonal across his forehead. He spread his hands and managed a clumsy smile.

"Somebody was murdered? Why didn't you say so, Lieutenant? I have nothing to hide."

"That's better. Much better."

"Do I know the victim?"

"You know him. Fred Duncan."

Strobe's face closed up against us in a sudden withdrawal. He stood, guardedly silent.

"Did you see Duncan last night?" Nola asked.

"No, sir."

"Yesterday at all?"

"During the afternoon."

"Where?"

"At his place of employment, the Merchant's Trust."

"And before that?"

"Not for a good many years."

"I understand he worked under you on a detail assigned to the District Attorney's office some time back."

"That's right."

"You knew him when he was pensioned off the force?"

"Yes, sir. After a bullet wound incapacitated him."

"And except for yesterday you had not seen him since that time."

"That is correct." Strobe's eyes were veiled and wary.

"Would you tell me why, Sergeant, after all these years of separation, on the afternoon of the day Duncan was murdered, you suddenly decide to renew your acquaintance?"

Strobe threw me a poisonous look. He knew that I had linked his name with Duncan's. He knew, too, that it would be pointless to squirm around known facts. He spoke evenly, choosing his words with care.

"Duncan needed money. Apparently he didn't care how he got it. So he wrote a book about the Keller suicide. Only he didn't call it a suicide. He invented a pack of lies about police bribery and conspiracy and murder. Somehow, his agent managed to palm it off on a gullible Hollywood producer as the truth. I myself was personally involved in that incident. My reputation was at stake, and the reputation of the men under me, of the department itself."

"The department will survive."

"I'm sure of that. Nevertheless I couldn't take it sitting down. So I went to see him. I wanted to talk it over, maybe straighten him out."

"With what results?"

"Better than I expected. He listened to reason. The money had already been paid to his agents, but he never got it. He said it had been stolen and he had nothing further to lose. He was willing to renege on the whole deal, admit his fraud, confess the book was a hoax."

"Oh, brother!" I said. "This character is good. He's wonderful. The most accomplished liar since Baron von Münchhausen."

"What's that?" Strobe's fists were clenched threateningly.

"You heard me. You're a liar! I saw Duncan and I spoke to him. Nothing could shake him loose, no threat, no intimidation. He was ready to stick to his story no matter what happened."

Anger mottled Strobe's face, coarsening the skin. He lifted one of the clublike fists.

"Hold it!" Nola said sharply. "Fred Duncan is dead, Sergeant. Have you any proof that he backed down on the facts in his book?"

Strobe looked at him heavily. "Not facts, Lieutenant. Lies. Fantasies. As you say, the man is dead. I did not record his words."

"But I did," I said. "I got them down on paper in a sworn affidavit before he died. Which you well knew because I told you. And which I was lucky enough not to leave in my office."

"What does that mean?"

"It means that I still have it. It means that the man who called my secretary with a phony story and decoyed her away from the office couldn't find it."

"Are you accusing me?"

"Does the shoe fit?"

"Hold it," Nola broke in. He divided a grim look between us. "You never told me about that, Counselor."

"Look at the hour, Lieutenant. Lapse of memory."

"Tell me now."

I gave it to him briefly.

He stared for a long moment at Strobe. "We'll continue this in the morning, Sergeant. I want you in my office at eight sharp, understand?"

Without waiting for an answer he turned and strode briskly toward the door. I followed him. Outside, he paused beside the police car. "You'll never get a cab at this hour. Jump in. I'll drive you home."

17

How can one sleep with his thoughts in a ferment? Yet I resisted the lure of a barbiturate, afraid it would dull a brain whose clear functioning was imperative. I stopped tossing and lit a cigarette in the dark.

What had started as a simple lawsuit by Fred Duncan now had more angles than a geometry textbook. All I wanted was a dignified practice, corporation law and probate matters.

Well, I had my probate matter—with a nice fat dividend of homicide thrown in.

"No man is an island," the poet said. The bell tolls for everybody. And so the death of Ben Keller had stretched its shadow across the years to affect the lives of utter strangers, including me.

I thought of Adam, alone in jail, with the vast mechanism of the law implacably closing in on him. And where, I wondered, was Dan Varney with his stolen two hundred thousand dollars? How long would the money last? And was it worth being a fugitive for the rest of his life?

Sleep finally came as the first gray streaks of dawn slanted through the window. But it was a restless, nightmare sleep.

And it lasted only three hours before the doorbell intruded on my consciousness.

The doorbell, insistent, without letup, with the abrasive quality of a hacksaw. I was numb for several moments, unable to move, and then, saturated with weariness and creaking in every joint, I swung out of bed, slipped into a robe and padded to the door.

A glance through the peephole showed me an emergency gathering of relatives. Barbara and the Dodds. I opened the door and they waded in, all yapping at me simultaneously. Adam's arrest was front-page news. Gil Dodd had seen the papers when he reached his office this morning. And they had tried to ring me, without success.

"I disconnected the phone," I said.

Victoria was outraged. "What kind of lawyer are you? Lounging in bed all morning while Adam is rotting away in jail."

"It's only nine o'clock and I didn't get to sleep until six."

"Six?" Barbara's eyes had widened suspiciously. "But you left me at midnight."

"True," I said. "Adam called me after he was arrested. I spent most of the night at Homicide West, trying to convince the lieutenant in charge that Adam was innocent."

"But he's still in jail. Can't you get him out?"

"Not at the moment."

"How about a habeas corpus?" Gil Dodd put in. "I read in a law book that—"

"Look," I said testily. "I don't care what you read in a law book. A writ of habeas corpus is employed only where there's illegal restraint. Adam is not being illegally restrained. He was apprehended in his own automobile, transporting the body of a murdered man who had recently started a lawsuit against him. They have every right to hold him for the Grand Jury on the evidence now available."

"You mean you think he's guilty?" Victoria demanded, eyeing me as if I had suddenly sprouted a pair of horns.

"No. Not at all. I'm simply being realistic and stating facts. Now look, everybody, please, I'm only half-awake. Calm down. And give me a chance to wash my face. See that door, Barbara. Behind it there's a kitchen with a stove and a percolator. Brew some coffee, if you please. Black and strong. I'll be back in a couple of minutes."

I retired to the bathroom and performed the necessary ablutions and combed my hair. At least it made me look human, and the coffee might almost make me feel human. A cup or two might even equip me to face the combined onslaught.

Victoria, emphatically backed by her husband, felt that Adam was entitled to bail.

"They've booked him on suspicion of first-degree murder," I explained. "Under the circumstances, bail would be denied."

"Did you see him last night?" Barbara wanted to know.

"Yes. After they put the collar on him."

"What?" She looked horrified.

"A colloquialism," I said. "It means arrested."

"What did he say?" Dodd asked.

"He said he was innocent, that he was working late and found Duncan's body in the car when he came down from his office."

"If that's what Adam said," Victoria maintained staunchly, "it's the truth."

"Of course it is," Barbara agreed.

"All right," I said. "You believe him. Your sister believes him. And your brother-in-law believes him. But the police are not related to Adam, and neither is the District Attorney. Their attitude is not affected by loyalty or affection. They see only the facts. Adam claims he found a body but failed to report it. Instead he was caught trying to dispose of the remains. He was driving with a flat tire. The murder weapon was in his car. Those are facts."

"Facts can lie."

"No, Barbara. The wrong conclusions may be drawn, but the facts themselves don't lie."

"And how about you, Scott? Do you believe Adam?"

"That has nothing to do with it."

"Oh, yes, it has. Because if you don't believe him, if you're at all doubtful, then you're not the lawyer to handle his case. We'd have to find someone else."

"You're overwrought," I said, "so we'll let that pass. In the first place, Adam doesn't want another lawyer. In the second place, where are you going to find a stranger who will take him on blind faith. And third, I merely want you to see the picture in its proper focus. If I had—"

The telephone was ringing. I crossed over and got it and said hello.

"Jordan?"

"Speaking."

"Listen carefully, mister." The voice was muffled and harsh. "This is your first and last warning. Be smart. Forget the Keller case. Forget everything connected with it."

"Who is this?"

"Never mind. You got the message."

"Just a minute. Would you answer one question."

"Ask Fred Duncan."

"Fred Duncan is dead."

"Precisely. Stick your nose where it don't belong and you'll join him." The line went dead.

I hung up slowly, keeping my face averted from the family. Of one thing I was sure. Threats are made through fear. The knowledge was small consolation, however. A frightened man is a desperate man—and desperation evokes violence.

What more proof did I need than Duncan's body on a slab in the morgue?

Barbara was watching me curiously. I shrugged negligently. "Nothing important."

Dodd said, "I think we ought to apologize, Jordan. We didn't mean to descend on you like this, but the emotional strain. . . ."

I waved it aside.

"Tell us this," he went on. "Did you accomplish anything at all last night?"

"Yes. I convinced Lieutenant Nola that other people besides Adam had a motive for killing Duncan. The machinery is in motion now and at least they'll check out other prospects."

"Who, for instance?"

"Ernie Strobe." I told them about our visit and it gave them a ray of hope.

"I don't suppose there's anything we can do about the publicity," Victoria said. "This may ruin Adam's agency."

"So what?" Barbara gave her a look. "The important thing is to clear Adam of a murder charge."

"Absolutely," Dodd agreed. "Is there anything we can do to help, Jordan?"

"Not at the moment. But I won't hesitate to call on any of you if I need to."

There was a moment of silence. Then Victoria cleared her throat and looked at me with faint embarrassment. Her concern for Adam had not erased other considerations and she could not refrain from asking about them.

"Have you, er, heard from that woman again?"

"Your stepmother? No. But I'm sure they're not sitting still."

"If she ever gets her claws on dad's estate, she'll rob it blind."

"Not if we demand the posting of a bond."

"What kind of a bond?"

"Assuring distribution of your father's estate under the law. She can legally claim one-third and we'll limit her to that."

"Unless she finds the will," Dodd said.

"Or two reliable witnesses," I reminded him, "who can testify to its contents."

He nodded, glanced at his watch, and turned to remind his wife that he had a business to run. He made motions of departure and she rose with him. Barbara seemed undecided and I told her to go along, promising to reach her later in the day.

When the door closed behind them, I called the office. Cassidy answered sharply until she recognized my voice. "I saw the papers," she said.

"Any calls?"

"Are you serious? We may have to install a switchboard for the journalists alone. Mostly requests for information and one offer of a fee for the inside story. How about an interview for NBC? On film for tonight's newscast."

"Not a chance."

"Marvelous publicity, Scott. Nationwide hookup on the whole network. You can build a new kind of practice."

"Yeah. How about Lieutenant Nola? Has he phoned?"

"Not yet. He's probably looking for a murderer. Max Turner tried you a little while ago. He's waiting at his office for you to call back."

"All right," I said. "I'll keep in touch."

I depressed the lever, got a dial tone, and then rang Max. "Anything special?" I asked him.

"Not yet. I read about Coleman and thought you might need me."

"I do, Max. I do. That list of cops I gave you, forget about them for the time being and concentrate on Strobe. Sergeant Ernie Strobe, attached to the Rackets Squad. Get everything you can. Outside associates, extracurricular activities, finances, and especially his activities last night. And be careful, Max. He's a bad actor."

Max promised to go to work at once. We broke the connection and I dialed Nola.

"How was your session with Strobe this morning?"

"We're still working on him."

"John, I'd like to have a chat with Fred Duncan's daughter-in-law. Would you give me her address?"

He checked it and relayed the information.

18

Ruth Duncan lived in the East Seventies, on one of those anomalous blocks where cold-water flats rub elbows with an occasional luxury apartment. I climbed three flights of narrow stairway and found her bell.

The door was opened by a small boy, under four years old, thin and spindly, with a pale face dominated by luminous eyes that studied me with intent curiosity.

"Good morning," I said.

"Who are you?" he asked with a child's directness.

"Scott Jordan."

"My name is Peter."

"How do you do, Peter."

"Are you another policeman?"

"Not exactly."

"There were two policemen here this morning. They talked to mama about grandpa. He used to be a policeman, too, before he worked in a bank. Did you know that?"

"Yes, Peter."

"He's dead now. They told mama and she cried a little. Did you know my grandpa?"

"Not very well."

"He took me to the zoo last week. We ate popcorn and frankfurters."

"They're my favorite for zoos."

"Mine, too."

"Your grandpa was a fine man."

"I know. Mama says all old people have to die sometime. I don't see why."

"They have to make room for little boys. Otherwise all the houses and the streets and the offices and everything would be too crowded."

He puzzled over that for a moment and then nodded solemnly.

"Where is your mama now?" I asked.

"Down in the basement with that old laundry machine. What do you want to see her about?"

"Just to talk."

"You can wait here if you like. She'll be up soon."

"Thank you, Peter."

He showed me into a small living room, worn but fastidiously neat. Furniture springs sagged and several bald spots were developing in the mohair upholstery. On the mantel was an enlarged photograph of a bony-faced young man with an uncertain smile. Its resemblance to the boy was unmistakable.

"That's my daddy," Peter said.

I nodded silently.

"He's dead, too. Mama says I'm the man in the family now."

"That's a great honor."

"I know." He was very solemn. "I like you."

"I like you too, Peter."

"Would you like to see my coloring set?"

"That would be fun."

"Then you have to come into the kitchen. I'm not allowed...."

He stopped because the door opened and a woman entered carrying a basket piled high with laundry. A little girl with enormous eyes trailed along hanging onto her skirt.

There was a pull of worry and resignation at her mouth as she put the basket down. "Oh, Lord, more questions."

"I'm not a detective, Mrs. Duncan."

She looked at me, frowning, a slender woman with a careworn face and tired eyes. Her mouth was soft, yet proud at the same time.

"I'm a lawyer," I said. "My name is Jordan—Scott Jordan."

She turned at once to the boy. "Peter, dear, take Linda into the kitchen and play with your coloring set. Finish the elephant. And remember what you saw at the zoo. His tusks were white, not green."

No insurrection. He was one of those rare children who obey unquestioningly. He gave me a smile, reached for his sister's hand and tugged her through the door.

Ruth Duncan regarded me openly. "You're the lawyer for the other side, aren't you?"

"It's not quite that simple."

"What do you mean?"

"In an odd kind of way, I'm really on both sides. I'm trying to find the man who stole Fred's money. And if I do find him, I intend to see that it is paid to Fred's legitimate heirs. Your children, most likely."

She stood, dubious and uncertain.

"Some people don't trust lawyers," I said. "They have the impression we're a devious breed. If you have any doubts about my intentions or my integrity, I suggest you call Fred's lawyer, Irving Birnbaum. Or check with Lieutenant John Nola at Homicide West. He's in charge of the investigation on. . . what happened last night. As a matter of fact, he's the man who gave me your address."

She shook her head slowly. "I don't believe it's necessary to call anyone. Fred mentioned your name several times. I think he trusted you."

"You know that he signed an affidavit at my request."

"Yes, he told me."

"Did he also tell you anything about Ernie Strobe?"

Her lips tightened and she averted her eyes.

"Please, Mrs. Duncan. This is no time for silence."

She thought a moment and reached a reluctant decision, speaking with an effort. "He said that Sergeant Strobe had threatened him."

"Where?"

"At the bank. Yesterday. Strobe went there and told Fred he'd better admit the book was a hoax or he'd never live to enjoy the money." She paused to get her lips under control. "Well, he didn't even live long enough to get the money."

"Did you tell this to Lieutenant Nola?"

She shook her head.

"Why not?"

"I didn't think it was important, not after the way they found Fred in that man's automobile. . . ."

"I think Adam Coleman is innocent, Mrs. Duncan. And Strobe had an entirely different version of his encounter with Fred. He said Fred agreed to recant, to admit the book was fiction, based on lies."

She bristled with indignation. "That's not true. Fred never made such a statement. He put everything down exactly as it happened."

"Will you swear to that, if necessary?"

"Of course."

"And he told you all about his book?"

"He didn't have to. He wrote it in longhand and I did the typing." She smiled wryly. "Fred wasn't very good at spelling and his sentence structure.... Well, I did what I could. I'm not a professional. But he insisted on paying me. Fifty cents a page. He knew I could use the money and how I hated to take charity—even from him."

"He never discussed the main event, the night Keller was killed?"

"Not until he started writing the book. And then I realized how much it bothered him. He knew he should have spoken up at the time and he was disgusted with himself for being a coward. But he was trapped by the system and he was trying to avoid trouble. He was afraid of losing his job. But then he lost it anyway. I know a lot of people thought he was sour and bitter because of the way it happened. And I suppose he was. It was so needless, so unfair.

"But there was a soft side to him, too. He loved the kids, Peter and Linda. And he was determined to make a life for them. I'm not sure he would ever have written the book if not for them. He didn't want the money for himself. His salary and pension more than covered his personal needs. But he felt the kids ought to have an education and a decent start. He was going to invest the two hundred thousand dollars in a trust for them."

Tears stung her eyes and she shook her head violently.

"No one knew Fred better than I. We were both lonely and he spent a lot of time here, talking. If he made up that story about Keller, I'd know it. Every word he wrote was true. Why do you think he never got any of that bribery money? Because they knew he wouldn't take it."

"You never met Strobe?"

"No." She swallowed and bit her lip, holding back.

"What is it, Mrs. Duncan? I think you'd better tell me."

She hungered for a sympathetic ear and the words came swiftly. "It—it may have been Strobe who called yesterday."

"About what?"

"About the kids. He said if I loved them, if I didn't want anything to happen to them, and if I had any influence with Fred, I'd make him back down on all that stuff he wrote in his book."

"You didn't recognize the voice?"

"No. I'd never heard it before."

"What time?"

"Around three in the afternoon."

"Did you tell Fred?"

"Yes. He was here for dinner last night. He said it was a bluff, but I could see he was worried. And he didn't want to take any chances. He had some money saved up and he wanted to send me and the kids away until this whole thing blew over. We were going to leave tomorrow. Fred said he knew a place upstate where we could rent a bungalow at this time of year for practically nothing. And he thought it would be good for the kids to get away from the city. But then. . . . '' Her voice dribbled away.

"What time did Fred leave here last night?"

"About nine. I had gone upstairs to borrow a valise from one of the neighbors and when I came down he was waiting with his hat on. He seemed to be in a hurry."

"Did he say where he was going?"

"No. But he seemed a little excited. Linda was in bed, sleeping. He rubbed Peter's head and left."

I stood up. "You've been very helpful, Mrs. Duncan. I don't want to make any promises about that money but, well, let's wait and see."

She managed a small smile.

"Say goodbye to Peter for me."

I stopped off at Schrafft's and sent the kids a five-pound box of candy. An occasional luxury is good for the soul. As it turned out, it was one of the best investments I ever made.

19

THE DISTRICT ATTORNEY'S OFFICE occupied four floors in the Criminal Courts Building, with the Homicide Bureau on the sixth. Up here the windows can be raised only three inches, on the principle that people charged with murder would rather take their chances on a six-floor jump than face a jury of their peers.

Assistant District Attorney Ed Magowan had consented to see me, but there was no pleasure in his greeting. Magowan had come a long way since we first crossed swords. He knew the ropes now. Seven years of practical experience had given him an air of competent assurance. He'd learned how to keep his voice and temper under control.

But he still had the manner of a junior-type executive. And he looked the part, too, with his neatly styled hair, his Brooks Brothers suit, and his bench-made mahogany-colored shoes. He kept his desk as neat as his person, clear of accumulated files and reference books.

"I suppose you're here about Adam Coleman," he said.

"That's right."

"You've got a tough one this time, Jordan."

"It looks worse than it is."

He smiled thinly. "Which makes it easier to get a conviction."

"We're a long way from any trial. When do you expect the Grand Jury to consider his case?"

"That's up to the Indictment Bureau. They're collecting evidence for presentation now." He regarded me shrewdly. "What's on your mind, Jordan?"

"I'd like to make an application for Coleman's release on bail."

"Go ahead," he said with casual unconcern.

"Will you oppose it?"

"Hell, yes."

"But you haven't got enough evidence."

"Perhaps not enough to convict at this time. Certainly enough to hold him. And we'll collect more."

I said, "Two weeks ago you made a speech at the Bar Association dinner."

"You heard me?"

"I was there. And I remember your words. You said the job of the District Attorney was to prosecute, not to persecute. You said the present administration was interested more in justice than a good record of convictions. Was that pure rhetoric, Magowan? For newspaper consumption? Or did you mean it?"

He gave me a politician's answer that committed him to nothing. "Look at the record. It speaks for itself."

"All right. Then we're both interested in the same thing. Justice. If you don't argue against bail, if Coleman is released, whoever killed Fred Duncan will think you have a weak case. He may be tempted to strengthen it. Every move he makes gives me an opportunity to nose him out."

"You?"

"The police," I amended.

He wore a set smile. "Your reasoning is based on a premise of innocence. I'm not convinced of that by any means. And in the meantime we have to hold him. The purpose of imprisonment is not to punish but to insure attendance at the trial."

"Exactly. Adam Coleman won't take a powder. He's no Bowery drifter. His home is here. He operates a business in this city."

"I'm aware of all that."

"And you're aware of the law, too. The power to grant bail by a Supreme Court justice, even in homicide cases, is discretionary."

His forensic skill had improved and he enjoyed displaying it.

" 'Unless the presumption is evident or the proof is great.' *People* v. *Perry*. There may not be an evident presumption here, but there certainly is considerable proof." He leaned forward confidentially. "Quite frankly, Jordan, I discussed this with the D.A. himself and he made the ruling. He wants Coleman in custody until we know what happened to the accused's partner."

"Dan Varney?"

"Yes."

"That's simple enough. Varney absconded with two hundred thousand dollars of Fred Duncan's money."

"So Coleman says. We have only his unsupported story."

I sat up. "What does that mean?" I said, knowing perfectly well what it meant.

"Can't you guess?"

"I want to hear you say it."

"Coleman may have stolen the money himself and done away with Varney as a blind."

"My God! You don't really believe that, do you?"

"The possibility exists and we haven't eliminated it."

"But he'd still be responsible to Duncan for the money."

"He didn't know that at the time. He's not a lawyer."

I shrugged. "If your thinking runs along those lines, I guess there's no point in discussing it."

"No point at all."

"Suppose I make an application for bail anyway."

"That's your privilege. We'll fight it out right down the line."

I could expect no leniency here and I rose to leave. Ed Magowan was still smiling as I went through the door. I stayed in the building and headed for the detention cells.

On the application of his attorney, they brought Adam out to the counsel room. He was nervous and rumpled, with a dark beard shadow on his face. He clutched at my sleeve.

"Get me out of here, Scott."

"I'm trying," I said. "It's not easy."

"Why? Don't we have a right to bail?"

"Not where a capital offense is involved."

"Even if I'm innocent?"

"We have to prove that first."

His mouth was pulled down at the corners. "Have you seen the family?"

"This morning."

"What does Barbara think?"

"She's in a fighting mood. And so is Victoria."

He nodded dismally. "Well, there goes the agency. With nobody at the office it can't last."

"How about Dodd? Doesn't he know anything about the business?"

"Gil is our accountant."

"Why not let him go through the mail? He can handle routine matters and let me know about emergencies."

Adam perked up a little. "Good idea. But they took my keys away."

"We'll get them back."

He searched my face. "I know you're not a magician, Scott. This thing only happened last night. But I . . . have you done anything yet?"

"Several things. I spoke to Fred Duncan's daughter-in-law this morning. She says he had an appointment last night. She doesn't know with whom, but I'm hoping to find out. I spoke to Lieutenant Nola and he's keeping an open mind. I have Max Turner checking on Ernie Strobe. You've got a lot of people in your corner, Adam. Everything possible is being done and will continue to be done. Just be patient."

We arranged to get his keys from the property clerk and they returned Adam to his cell. When I left the property clerk's office I went down to the lobby and used a telephone booth to call the office.

"High time you phoned," Cassidy said. "There's an envelope here from the Bar Association, delivered by hand!"

"Open it."

I heard the rustle of paper, silence for a moment, and then Cassidy's voice, subdued.

"Do you know a Mr. Alfred Seward?"

"Not offhand."

"He represents the Grievance Committee. A complaint has been filed against you by Mrs. Lorraine Coleman, charging unethical conduct in the suppression of a testamentary document. He would like you to phone him at your earliest convenience."

My blood pressure skyrocketed. Angry words rushed to the tip of my tongue, most of them attacking Mrs. Coleman, attacking her ancestry and her lawyer, too.

"Are you there, Scott?"

"Yes. Seward, did you say?"

"Alfred Seward."

"Look, Cassidy. Two can play at this game. The lady wants trouble, we'll give it to her. Meet me at my apartment and bring some legal cap. About seven."

20

LORRAINE COLEMAN undoubtedly knew of Adam's
plight. It was in all the newspapers. She knew, too,
that I was defending him. But how could I concentrate with this added load? And just what did she
hope to accomplish by a personal attack on my professional conduct?

A complaint to the Grievance Committee was
unnerving. If I could not satisfy Seward of my innocence, if formal charges were filed with the Executive Committee, I might ultimately wind up before
the Appellate Division with my career at stake. This
thing had to be nipped in the bud.

The Bar Association was housed in a building on
West Fifty-fourth Street. I had called Alfred
Seward and arranged for an appointment. Then I
made a few other calls and got a line on the man. He
was a permanent member of the staff, a little
starchy perhaps, but fair and impartial.

A secretary showed me into his office.

He sat behind his desk, tall and angular, with a
brushcut mustache and direct blue eyes. He wore a
high, stiff collar and an undertaker's suit. He
offered me a formal handshake, a hard-backed
chair and a cigarette. Then he settled back, care-

fully hiked up a trouser leg and crossed his knees and studied me carefully.

"You understand, Jordan, this is not a formal hearing. As counsel for the committee my job is to process the complaint and decide what further measures should be taken. I am merely asking you at this time to explain the charges."

We were two gentlemen politely discussing a problem. No inquisitorial aspect. Nobody's professional ethics in question. If a lawyer had to be crucified, Seward would officiate with elegance and finesse.

"What, precisely, are the charges?" I asked.

He outlined them in a matter-of-fact tone. "Mrs. Coleman claims that you had a copy of her husband's will in your office, that she asked you to file it with the surrogate, that you not only neglected to do so, but instead destroyed the document or disposed of it in some other manner."

"And my reasons for doing this?"

"Twofold. To deprive her of the full estate and for your own personal gain."

"Just how would I stand to gain, Mr. Seward?"

"Through your clients. Adam Coleman, Barbara Coleman and Victoria Dodd. Between them, if no will were found, they may inherit close to three million dollars. Your fee for handling an estate of that size would be quite substantial."

"May I talk off the record, sir?"

"If you wish."

"All right. The complainant first. Lorraine Coleman is a greedy, acquisitive woman. Her marriage to M. Parker Coleman, a man thirty years her senior,

not in good health even then, was coldly and cal-
culatingly manipulated. She married the man for his
money. She influenced him in a decision to disinherit
his own children. All she had to do was wait.

"Her husband, however, refused to cooperate.
Dying was a slow process and she squandered a good
portion of her youth. Last week, Mr. Coleman finally
obliged. At last his money came within reach. But
suddenly she is faced with a new hazard. She can't
find the will. So she comes to me for a copy. That,
too, appears to be missing. Imagine her frustration,
the paranoiac delusion that she's being cheated, her
blind, unreasoning anger.

"So she strikes out wildly at the nearest target,
the man she believes is scheming against her. She
selects me as the villain because offhand she has no
one else. And her distorted brain must have some
victim."

Seward's bottom lip bulged thoughtfully behind
his tongue.

"A rather merciless indictment, Counselor."

"It has validity. Something her charges lack."

"Who drew the will?"

"Oliver Wendell Rogers."

"Ah, yes. A decided asset to the Bar. He's retired
now, isn't he?"

"Yes, sir. I was his junior for several years."

"Where can he be reached?"

"I don't know. He's traveling around Europe on a
vacation."

"Who were the attesting witnesses?"

"His former secretary, now employed by me, and
myself."

"Did your files ever contain a copy of the will?"

"I don't know. I never saw one."

"And you deny any knowledge of such a copy."

"I deny it categorically and unequivocally. May I suggest another approach to this problem?"

He dipped his chin one millimeter.

I said, "Why is Mrs. Coleman concentrating exclusively on a copy of the will? The answer is obvious. Because the original is missing. Well, sir, no one suggests that I had any control over that particular document. Nevertheless it cannot be found. Under the circumstances, what is the normal assumption? That Mr. Coleman himself destroyed it. That he had second thoughts about disinheriting his children. That he had feelings of guilt and revoked his will without telling his wife. That he contacted Rogers with instructions to destroy the copy."

"Mrs. Coleman refuses to believe that."

"Mrs. Coleman believes only what she wants to believe—whatever serves her own self-interest."

"You're a persuasive young man."

"No, sir. My arguments are persuasive because they're logical."

He leaned forward, pinching his lower lip reflectively. "Is there any way we can test or nourish your hypothesis by getting in touch with Rogers?"

"I'm afraid not. He has no particular itinerary."

"How long will he be gone?"

"I'm not sure. Mrs. Coleman would have to wait his return in any event."

"What do you mean?"

"The precedent is established, sir. A lost will may be probated if its provisions are clearly and distinctly proved by two credible witnesses."

"Or one witness and a copy, I believe."

"Yes, sir. But there is no copy."

"I see your point." He stroked his mustache. "How does Mrs. Coleman get along with her step-children?"

"They abominate her and the feeling is mutual. They know why she married their father, and they watched her reduce him to a simpering adolescence. They felt she had alienated his affections and was trying to deprive them of their inheritance. And she in turn believes they're trying to bilk her out of the estate."

"Are they?"

"No, sir. Emphatically not."

"But they want their share."

"They're entitled to it, Mr. Seward. But they never came to me and suggested that I act unethically or illegally in their behalf. Nor would I have done so. My record as a member of the Bar proves that."

He pursed his lips noncommittally. He was squaring some papers on his desk and sliding them back into a folder.

He said, "There are several items I want to run down before making any recommendation to the Executive Committee. Thank you for coming, Counselor. You'll hear from us."

So the interview was over and I had no hint where I stood. Seward did not rise to offer his hand when I left. Perhaps I had pushed too hard. Or perhaps he'd found my explanation not quite satisfactory enough.

Going down in the elevator, I thought of Lorraine Coleman with a sharpened barometric sensitivity. I itched to feel the lady's neck between my fingers. And I had a sense of identity with Barbara in her aversion for Lorraine.

I glanced at my watch. It was almost six, too late to go back to the office. I caught a cab home and sank wearily into a chair. The light was fading and shadows lengthened across the room. I let this moment of calm engulf me and then I remembered that Cassidy was due.

I took a quick shower and was in a robe when the bell rang. I let her in. She surveyed me with a lifted eyebrow.

"Aren't we supposed to work this evening?"

"Yes."

"Do you always greet female employees in a robe?"

"What's the matter? Worried about your reputation?"

"At my age? Ha! Where's the portable?"

I went to the hall closet, got the typewriter and set it up on the living-room desk. "Hope you brought a new ribbon."

"As a matter of fact, I did." She fussed over the machine. "The hours I work. And no overtime."

"Think of your Christmas bonus. If this case pans out I'll buy you a vacation at Miami Beach."

"I wouldn't be found there dead."

"Pick your own spot."

"Bermuda."

"It's a deal."

She turned from the typewriter, opened a large manila envelope, withdrew some legal cap and a steno pad. "How did you make out with Seward at the Bar Association?"

"I don't know. Mrs. Coleman accused us of conspiracy. I denied the charge and he's taking it under advisement. That's why you're here. We'll give the widow something to worry about. We're going to draw papers tonight, an application for letters of administration in her husband's estate. We'll ask to have the children appointed. Naturally she'll hit the ceiling. And immediately she'll file a cross-application.''

"She's the widow. She has a right to be administrator."

"True. But I want to get her started. Let her produce a will for probate or proceed under the rules of intestacy.''

I started to dictate and the phone rang. Cassidy reached for it out of habit and said, "Hello," then handed it to me.

It was Barbara, coolly aloof. "Am I interrupting something?"

"Don't jump to conclusions," I said. "I am not a philanderer. That female voice you just heard was my secretary. We're working. On Coleman family business, as a matter of fact.''

She was mollified and hurt at the same time. "You promised to call me."

"Sorry. Things have been popping all day. Your lovely stepmother filed a complaint against me with the Bar Association.''

"Oh, Scott! Is it serious?"

"I'm not sure. Expressions of sympathy are welcome.''

"I have an oversupply. Take me to dinner.''

"Soon as I finish with Cassidy. I want to serve these papers first thing in the morning. I'll call you before I leave.''

"I'm at Vickie's," she said. "The phone number's 555-0010. Did you see Adam?"

"Yes. I'll tell you about it later." I had a second thought. "Look, this won't take long. Cassidy knows the forms pretty well. Let's save time. Meet me at Larue's in half an hour."

"I'll be at the bar," she said and hung up.

"Why didn't you tell me?" Cassidy asked. "I could have brought a set of blank forms from the office."

"Because I forgot. And besides, I keep a fairly complete set here at the apartment. Let's go to work." I dictated the essential points and outlined the rest.

The phone rang again. I took it myself and heard John Nola's voice. "They're moving fast, Scott. Just got a notification to appear before the Grand Jury tomorrow afternoon."

"The Duncan case?"

"Yes. They're asking for a murder one indictment."

"That's what I expected, but it's a far cry from an indictment to a conviction."

"Just thought I'd let you know."

"I appreciate it, John. Thanks." We broke the connection.

"What is it now?" Cassidy asked.

"The District Attorney is wasting no time. I wonder if they found any additional evidence."

"You look worried."

"I am. Adam may not have told me the whole truth."

"You'll find out after the Grand Jury meets."

"Provided I get my hands on a copy of the minutes, which is highly improbable."

"How about those surrogate forms? Where are they?"

It took me about ten minutes to find them and then I stood over Cassidy, watching her fill in the title. She pointed at the clock. "Half an hour, did you say? It's after that now. Your date will be fuming."

"My God!" I said. "You're right. I have to dash."

"Not in that robe. Put some clothes on first. And I think you need a shave."

I rubbed my jaw and felt the rasp of a beard stubble. Heading for the bathroom, I said over my shoulder, "Call the restaurant and tell Miss Barbara Coleman that I'll be delayed a short while."

I worked up a lather and put a fresh blade into the razor. I had finished scraping and was in the bedroom selecting haberdashery when the doorbell rang.

I looked out. "Answer that, will you, Cassidy?"

She stopped typing. I went to the rack and found a tie, dark maroon, and slipped it under my shirt collar, carefully knotting it.

I heard a heavy thump.

"Who is it, Cassidy?"

No answer. Not a sound.

I frowned in puzzlement and went to the living room. She was not there.

"Cassidy?"

No response.

I crossed to the foyer and stopped rigidly. Cassidy lay, face down, in a grotesque position on the floor. My scalp tightened and I dropped to one knee beside her. A burnt powder smell hung in the air. I touched her arm. It was inert, motionless. I turned her over and saw the bullet hole.

I thought I was going to be sick, but shock froze my stomach and my reflexes. I kneeled there, numb and paralyzed. It was a ghastly sight. She had opened the peephole for a look at the visitor. There had been no warning. The gun was in position, waiting, silenced and lethal, and a bullet had exploded through Cassidy's brain.

My eyes were burning and my throat ached and I cried her name in a lost and stricken voice.

21

I HAVE ONLY A DAZED recollection of the next few hours, a stunned awareness of kaleidoscopic activity. Sirens in the night, the arrival of John Nola, a parade of technicians, flashbulbs and fingerprint powder, the medical examiner, stretcher bearers from the morgue, neighbors being questioned, reporters clamoring.

Why? I kept asking myself. Why?

This was a macabre jest, some monstrous hoax. Part of me refused to accept the fact, and yet I knew it had to be so. There had been a war in my time. I had seen death in many and various forms. But Cassidy had been a part of my life, a part of my everyday existence.

Everyone had left now. Only Nola remained. He went to the bar, poured a double shot of brandy, and put it in my hand. "Drink that."

I put it down in a single gulp.

He stood over me, eyes leveled at mine. "I understand your feelings, Scott, and I sympathize with them. I know what Cassidy meant to you. All right. Mourn for her. But right now pull yourself together. I need your help."

"She was here working," I said heavily.

"We saw the copy in your typewriter."

"Somebody rang the bell and she went to answer. She caught it when she looked through the peephole."

"Where were you when it happened?"

"In the bedroom getting dressed—" I stopped, remembering my appointment with Barbara.

Nola read my thought. "Miss Coleman phoned and I explained the situation. She wanted to come right over, but I told her to go home, you'd be in touch with her."

I looked up at him. "Cassidy never had a chance."

"How long did it take you to get to the door?"

"Two, three minutes."

"Didn't you hear the shot?"

"No."

"Neither did the neighbors. The gun had a silencer."

"Why, John? What did anybody have against Cassidy?"

"Nothing probably." He stared at me. "Don't you see the implication, Scott?"

I shook my head.

"That packet carried your name. It was delivered to the wrong party. The killer didn't know he was firing at Cassidy. He couldn't see her face through the peephole."

Nola was right, of course. The killer had expected me to be alone, had been certain there was no margin for error. And hardly any risk. Who else but the tenant would answer a bell. A quick twitch of the trigger and the job is done. So Cassidy, an innocent bystander, had died. Bitter saliva threaded its way down my throat.

"Any ideas, Counselor?"

"It's tied up with the Duncan case."

"Fill me in."

"I had a threatening call, John, warning me to keep my nose out of it. And to forget the Keller business. Somebody has an idea I'm getting too close for comfort."

"Where do you keep your gun?"

"I beg your pardon."

"Your gun. Three years ago I got you a license to carry a firearm. I know it's been renewed. Where do you keep the piece?"

"In a shoebag compartment."

"See if it's still there."

I found it, a Colt Banker's Special, caliber .32, small but lethal enough at close range.

"Keep it handy," Nola said. "I want you to carry it around until this case is settled one way or another."

"I'm a lawyer, John, not a perambulating arsenal."

"You used similar words once before, but it saved your life. There's a killer abroad, remember?" His voice hardened. "I suggest that gun because your life is in danger. As an instrument of self-defense, not revenge. Am I clear?"

"Would you deny me the pleasure, John?"

"Yes. Punishment is not your job, nor mine either."

I committed myself to nothing by changing the subject. "What about Ernie Strobe?"

"We're still checking. He's well fixed financially. So far we've uncovered about eighty thousand in securities."

"Pretty good on a sergeant's salary. How long before you clamp down?"

"The decision is not mine to make." He regarded me speculatively. "Did you know you had a visitor this evening?"

"Who?"

"Mrs. M. Parker Coleman."

I gaped at him. "Where was I?"

"In the bedroom being questioned. She figured something had happened from all the activity but insisted on seeing you anyway, so we let her in."

"What happened?"

"Well, the body was still here. She took one look and passed out. When she came to she was on the verge of hysterics. The medical examiner had just arrived and he put her under sedation. I had one of the boys drive her home."

"I wonder what she wanted," I mused.

"The doc said to give her a couple of hours." He glanced at his watch. "It's about time that shot wore off. Would you like to come along?"

"Try to stop me."

Before relinquishing control of the Coleman Hotels, M. Parker Coleman had signed over to himself a long-term lease for a duplex in the Marlborough—at a bargain rental, no doubt. It had been furnished in Danish modern and carried the earmarks of liberal spending. Masons had broken through the living-room wall to create a twenty-foot picture window that commanded a view of Central Park with its constantly changing panorama.

A middle-aged housekeeper with a knotty face seemed shocked at our late visit. She had a devout impression the Coleman privacy was inviolable, but Lieutenant Nola's curt air of authority put her straight and she retired, grumbling audibly, to rouse her mistress.

Lorraine Coleman looked drawn, her eyes slightly drugged. She greeted us stiffly in a hostess gown of whispering taffeta.

"Sorry to disturb you at this hour," Nola said. "But we have to move fast in a homicide investigation."

"I understand." She gestured in my direction. "Is he part of the investigation?"

"Jordan is involved. The victim was his secretary."

No expression on her face, nor any comment.

"We believe she was killed by mistake. The bullet was intended for Jordan."

"What has all this to do with me?"

"You arrived at the scene not long after it happened, Mrs. Coleman. The possibility exists that you went there earlier and were undecided about entering."

"The possibility is a fact," she said after a moment's hesitation. "I walked away twice before making up my mind."

The admission was not surprising. Lorraine Coleman was no fool. She realized someone might have seen her in the vicinity.

"Then you may be able to help us," Nola said. "Did you notice anyone loitering about the building?"

"No."

"Going in or coming out?"

"No."

"What brought you to Jordan's apartment?"

"I think he knows."

"Suppose you tell us, Mrs. Coleman."

"I went there with a request and an offer. I

believe Jordan knows where a copy of my husband's will can be found. I had spoken to him about it once before, but my approach was wrong. I thought if we discussed it reasonably he'd come over to my side."

"That was your request. What was your offer?"

"If he produced the will, I was ready to drop my complaint to the Bar Association."

"Plus how much money?" I asked.

"Money?" One eyebrow arched questioningly.

"Sure. Weren't you prepared to offer me more than I could make as a legitimate fee from my clients?"

"Not at all. I considered my original offer fair."

"And your lawyer," I said. "Did he know about this?"

"It was my own idea."

"Naturally. He knows my office is on the tenth floor. That's a lot of stairs to be kicked down."

It didn't touch her at all. Lorraine Coleman operated in a sphere of her own. She turned back to Nola. "Am I a suspect, Lieutenant?"

"Everyone is a suspect."

She encompassed her apartment with a regal wave. "Would you like to search for a gun?"

"A gun may be discarded. It's not permanently attached to your person."

"But my hand is." She held it out. "Isn't there some sort of test you make to determine if a gun has been fired?"

He smiled dryly. "Knowing about the test you would have worn gloves."

"Like any normally intelligent murderer—is that what you mean, Lieutenant?"

"In a way. I'm curious. How do you happen to know about such things?"

"I'm incurably addicted to mystery stories." Her eyes veered across the room to one of those handsome perpetual clocks that are powered by a two-degree change in temperature. "This has been a trying experience, Lieutenant. I'm very tired."

"Of course. We may have to question you again."

"You know my address. Good night." She retired peremptorily from the scene, leaving her housekeeper to perform the amenities.

Downstairs, Nola shook his head. "That's a tough combination to solve."

"She operates on the profit motive," I said. "The lady has a slide-rule personality with a money fixation. Everything she does can be figured in terms of the dollar gain on her side of the ledger."

He pursed his lips thoughtfully. "You may be right at that. Can I give you a lift?"

"No, John. Thanks anyway. I feel like walking.

Mostly, I didn't want to go back to the apartment. The night was crisp and clear, with an indigo sky and a sprinkling of stars. A view denied now to Cassidy. A view she would never see again.

I don't know how long I trudged the streets—two hours, three hours until, inevitably, I found myself in front of Barbara's apartment. I went in and rang her bell. The buzzer answered at once and I took the elevator up.

She was waiting at the door, her eyes searching my face with concern. "I knew you'd come," she said simply.

I nodded, wordless, and sank into a chair.

She stood in front of me. "Where is it all going to end, Scott?"

"I don't know."

"But why Cassidy? Why your secretary?"

"Her death was a mistake. The killer was after me."

"Oh, no!" She went rigid, fighting panic. Her fists were clenched in front of her. "Is it . . . is it because of Adam's case?"

I shrugged.

"Then drop it, Scott. We'll get someone else."

"No, Barbara. A man can't surrender to intimidation."

"But this is more than intimidation. These people are vicious killers. Two murders have been committed already." She looked at me beseechingly. "Leave town, Scott. Go away."

"And desert Adam?"

"But you're not the only lawyer in New York."

"Nor the best," I said. "But I know this case and I'm the one he wants."

After a moment, she nodded, looking miserable. "You're right, of course, I'm sorry." And added defensively, "But I'm frightened, too."

So was I, as a matter of fact, but I didn't put it into words. Merely considering the possible means of ambush was enough to chill my spine.

"Is there a connection between the two murders?" she asked.

"I'm sure of it."

Her fingers caught my arm. "Don't you see what that means?" she said excitedly. "Adam was in jail when Cassidy was shot. He was behind bars. He couldn't have been involved. And he had no motive for hurting you."

"Yes," I said. "I see what it means. But I don't

think the District Attorney will see it. Not yet anyway. He'd want proof.''

''Can we find any?''

''I have a private detective working on it.''

''The same man who's trying to find Dan?''

''Yes, with the help of assistants.''

She looked woebegone. ''We Colemans are a headache. Are you sorry to be involved with us?''

''You have legal problems. That's my trade.''

''But what if you're disbarred?''

''Then you can support me. How many productive years does a model have?''

She caught my bantering tone. ''Quite a few. Later on I can pose for gray-hair rinses, dental-plate cleansers, concealed hearing aids and—''

''That's enough,'' I interrupted. ''None of this may be necessary. As things now stand, you're in line to inherit quite a chunk of your father's estate.''

''I see. Then you're interested in me because I'm an heiress.'' Her face changed. ''Scott, you're not really going back to that apartment tonight, are you?''

''Is there an alternative?''

''You can stay here if you like.'' She made the offer simply and ingenuously. I looked at her in surprise and her cheeks colored. ''The sofa's very comfortable,'' she added.

''Give me a raincheck,'' I said. ''Going back tomorrow or next week won't make it any easier.''

I stood up and she clung to me a moment before letting me go.

22

In the morning, John Nola called me as I was leaving for the office. "Just heard some bad news," he said. "Thought I'd let you know."

"I'm immune by now. What happened, John?"

"Max Turner was taken to Roosevelt Hospital two hours ago. He was found in a hallway on Thirty-ninth Street with a possible brain concussion."

But I wasn't immune at all. My stomach shrank. I hung up without thinking. Max, I thought. Max, too. So the violence was spreading.

I reached for the phone to call Nola back and apologize. It started ringing.

"Hello."

"Jordan?"

"Yes."

"Ed Magowan. We want you down here at the D.A.'s office."

"Later," I said.

"*Now.*" His voice was sharp and peremptory. "Get down here at once or I'll send a man after—"

I cut him off. Unceremoniously. The thing was ringing again as I reached the door. I ignored it and went out.

When I reached the hospital I found Max in the men's ward. A white bandage circled his head like a turban. He was sitting up in bed with a thermometer in his mouth and a nurse taking his pulse. The nurse was young and her starched white uniform was helpless against a burgeoning figure. Max smiled at me beatifically.

"How is he?" I asked the nurse.

She removed the thermometer and held it up to the light.

"Almost normal." Her armor was a brisk, business-like manner. She lifted the chart from the foot of his bed, made a notation, and moved on to the next patient.

"Some dish," Max said, looking down his nose.

I knew then that his skull had absorbed the shock without damage. "How do you feel?"

"Fair. I'll be out of here tomorrow morning."

"What happened, Max?"

"Somebody clouted me from behind and dragged me into a hallway."

"Did Strobe know you were investigating him?"

"It was no secret. I've been all over town making inquiries. I told you about speaking to some of the men who were on duty with him that night at the hotel."

"That was only a warning, Max."

He nodded, suddenly sober.

"No point in sticking your neck out, Max. Shall I take you off the case?"

"You kidding?" He regarded me levelly. "Are *you* getting out, Counselor? After what happened to Cassidy?"

"No."

"Then count me in, too. Hell, word gets around that I scare easy, it's bad for business. Got to expect a little violence. Occupational hazard. Don't worry about me, Counselor. I'll be out of here tomorrow."

"Is there anything I can do, Max? Anything you need?"

"With a nurse like that on hand? Forget it."

I left him and went out to the street and flagged a cab. "Criminal Courts Building," I told the driver. I sat back and patted my pocket for the reassuring feel of my Banker's Special. There was a clicking noise and I put my hand in and came up with a set of strange keys. Then I remembered. They were the keys to Adam's office that he wanted delivered to Gil Dodd.

"Change of destination," I told the driver. "Forty-third Street and Sixth Avenue."

Why did I do it when I knew Magowan was waiting? And burning. Rebellion against authority, I suppose. Defiance against the soulless mechanism of bureaucracy. An expression of independence.

The driver had his eye on the rear-vision mirror. "I think somebody's following us."

"If it's a private car, get his number."

"It's a cab. Shall I try to shake him?"

"No," I said. "Let him tag along."

I had the fare ready when he pulled up. I got out, turned casually and watched the street. The first cab was empty and obviously cruising. The second had a passenger whose eyes were turned in my direction. I caught a blurred glimpse of a wide pale face surmounted by a dark homburg. The cab went past and turned the corner. I heard the squeal of brakes and knew it was discharging its passenger.

I waited, lighting a cigarette, until I saw the homburg over my cupped palms. Then I turned and en-

tered the building. The directory gave me Gil Dodd's
office number.

He had, I found, sublet space for himself and a girl
in the suite of a large accountancy firm. The place
was a beehive, with a window looking into a stenographic pool where typewriters and adding
machines were clicking at a furious rate.

With all the paperwork of modern business, with
the endless forms, the inventory control, purchasing
costs, production figures; with financing, advertising, sales, withholding taxes, excess profits, and
maybe even two sets of books, one for the company
and one for Internal Revenue, it struck me that if all
the accountants simultaneously went on strike, a
kind of mathematical anarchy would throw the in-
dustrial complex of the country into a hopeless
uproar.

Gil Dodd came to the reception room when my
name was announced. I got a sympathetic handshake, some commiserating remarks about Cassidy
and a personal escort back to his room. He offered
me a chair and sat behind his desk, shoving a pile of
papers to one side.

"What can I do for you, Jordan?"

"Not for me," I said. "For Adam." I dropped the
keys on his desk. "He's worried about the agency.
There may be some urgent business waiting at the office. He wants you to handle the mail, deposit checks
if any, make necessary phone calls, you know, keep
the operation rolling."

"Of course. It's been troubling me, too. I meant to
call you about it, but—" he gestured ruefully at the
papers on his desk "—I've been snowed under, what
with tax time approaching. I'll attend to it this after-

noon." He beetled his brows. "Barbara tells me that Lorraine filed a complaint against you with the Bar Association."

"It's true."

"Good heavens! On what grounds?"

"Conspiring with the family to gyp her out of some three million dollars."

He drew an incensed breath. "The woman's demented."

"Yeah," I said. "We'll have to tip off the Grievance Committee."

"Surely we can help. If there's a hearing we'll testify in your behalf."

"Anything the family says would be self-serving and about as effective as salad oil as a cure for gout."

He shook his head. "I don't understand that woman. She'll inherit a cool million under any circumstances. At six percent that's sixty thousand a year and she doesn't have to bite into the capital. Or she can invest in municipal bonds at four percent and get forty thousand. Tax free, too. Isn't that enough? Why pauperize the rest of the family?"

"Greed feeds itself," I said. "She's insatiable."

He nodded morosely. "Any trace of a will yet?"

"They haven't found one." An idea suddenly occurred to me. "Look, Dodd, perhaps old M.P. never put that will in his bank vault. Maybe he stored it in the safe at one of his hotels."

Dodd's brows contracted and he pinched his lips thoughtfully. "It's possible. I'd hate to believe it, though." He looked at me shrewdly. "Do you really want me to make such a check, Counselor?"

"Either you or Lorraine's lawyer."

"It won't help the family."

"It will help me. Lorraine would drop her charges. And incidentally it would serve justice."

"Are you going to suggest it to him?"

"Yes."

He lifted his shoulders in resignation. "I suppose it's the right thing to do. All right, if you insist, I'll contact the various managers."

"One other thing," I said. "While you're at Adam's office, see if you can find a copy of Duncan's manuscript. I'd like to read it."

He pushed resolutely away from his desk. "I'll attend to it right now."

We went down together and Dodd hailed a cab. Across the street I caught sight of a man in a dark homburg. He was turning to inspect the contents of a luggage shop. I was late for my appointment with Magowan, and I knew that I couldn't push the D.A.'s office too far. But once I got near the Criminal Courts Building I might lose my tail.

So Magowan would have to wait.

I started north, moving at a normal speed. Occasionally I stopped, ostensibly to do some window shopping. And each time I checked I found that my satellite was still in orbit. He was a man of average height, in a long gabardine coat of navy blue. And he knew his trade, keeping the proper distance, looking casual and unconcerned, working both sides of the street.

When he was directly behind me, the skin tightened around my temples.

I thought of Duncan's lifeless body propped up in Adam's car. I thought of a bullet hurtling through the peephole of my apartment door. I thought of a gun butt exploding against the back of Max Turner's skull, And, quite irrelevantly, I thought how various parts of the human anatomy behave differently under stress.

For my throat was dry and my hands wet.

Here on a Manhattan street, in broad daylight, with pedestrians on all sides, I felt safe enough. I could even chuck the whole thing. I could walk to the bank, draw my balance, shake my tail, and put some geography between myself and the impending danger.

Instead I ambled north. On Fifty-eighth Street I swung east. My apartment building goes clear through the block, with another entrance on Central Park South. I used the rear door, figuring it would draw him inside to make sure I did not leave at the other end.

I hurried to the self-service elevator. I reached a hand inside and touched the seventh-floor button. Then I stepped back and ducked out of sight around a bend in the corridor.

He plunged through the door and stopped at the elevator. His eyes went to the indicator hand and watched it stop at seven. He touched the button and waited for the car to come down. He stood there, a slope-shouldered man with grizzled hair at the back of his neck.

I took the Colt Banker's Special out of my pocket and released the safety catch.

23

I WAS RIGHT BEHIND HIM when the elevator door slid open. I helped him across, jabbing the gun against his back, crowding in after him.

"Don't move a muscle," I said. "Stand fast."

His spine was arched, elbows flaring away from his body like a pair of broken wings, fingers apart. I pushed the seventh-floor button again and backed away.

"Turn around," I said.

He faced me slowly, a lantern-jawed man with flat eyes under crimped brows. Smoke stains showed on his lower teeth behind the slack lip. He was not young. Up close, his skin had a rough, granular texture. There was a faint whistle in his breathing as if he had an obstruction against the bridge of his saddle-shaped nose. The colorless eyes were fixed on the Banker's Special.

"Don't sell it short," I said. "It's small but effective. Especially at this range."

He moistened his lips and spoke mildly. "No argument from me, my friend. Take my money and leave me alone. I won't even complain to the police."

Fast and nimble, I thought, and said, "But I want the police to be notified."

His brow wrinkled. "I don't understand. Isn't this a stickup?"

"Not quite."

The car glided to a stop and the doors opened. I gestured with my head.

"March," I said. "Out. And be very damn careful. This gun has a sensitive trigger and I'm extremely jittery at the moment."

"Look, friend—"

"I'm not your friend. Out. Turn right and walk to the end of the hall."

I let him get several paces beyond my apartment. I stopped him and keyed open the door. Then I called him back and gestured him in. I offered him my favorite chair, deep and soft, with down cushions and a reclining back. I was not being a gracious host. Altruism and benevolence had nothing to do with it. But any sudden movement from the chair is extremely awkward and heralded by a visible recruiting of muscles and joints.

I went around behind him. I put the cold muzzle of the gun against the nape of his neck. He froze instantly. I reached with my free hand and found an underarm holster under the lapel of his jacket, complete with cargo.

I stayed behind him and examined it. A Smith & Wesson .38 revolver. I broke it open, spun the barrel and saw that it was fully loaded. I released the safety and put my own gun in my pocket. With all this hardware I almost felt invincible.

I stood in front of him and drew a bead dead center between his eyes, wondering what ballistics could prove with a sample bullet fired from the .38. Would it match the slug that killed Cassidy? The man sat utterly motionless. Under the homburg, his face glistened with moisture.

"You understand that carrying a gun is a violation of the Sullivan Law," I said. "I hope you have a license. Otherwise you're guilty of a felony."

"So are you."

"Am I?"

"Yes, sir. Kidnapping. Abduction."

"Add another one," I said. "Assault and battery. I don't like being shadowed. Not by a man with a gun. Especially after somebody tried to kill me last night. I intend to find out why."

His hands rested on his knees and the flat eyes regarded me without expression.

"Who are you working for?" I asked.

"The City of New York."

I narrowed my eyes at him.

"That's right," he said. "The City of New York. I'm a police officer."

It set me back for a moment. I had a sudden pang of misgiving. He could have been detailed to keep an eye on me by Lieutenant Nola. The lieutenant wanted no more killings in his bailiwick.

"Where's your shield?"

"In my pocket."

"Take it out with your fingertips, slowly and carefully."

He bent forward, shifting his weight, and reached into his hip pocket. A black leather wallet appeared. He flipped it open, displaying the blue and gold shield of a city detective.

"Satisfied?"

"Who assigned you to this job?"

"What job?"

"Tailing me."

"You're mistaken, Counselor. I wasn't tailing you. I have no interest in you at all."

"I'm a total stranger?"

"That's right."

"Do you know my name?"

"No."

"And this whole incident is a misunderstanding."

"Seems that way."

"Boy!" I said regretfully. "I wish I had you on a witness stand. You're a bad liar. If I'm a total stranger, why did you call me Counselor? How did you know I'm a lawyer?"

He lifted his hand and deliberately massaged his chin, watching me, his face deadpan.

I sidled over to the desk and reached for the telephone. I dialed a number and asked for Lieutenant Nola. He came on at once.

"Scott? What's eating you, boy? The D.A.'s howling for blood. You were supposed to be in his office over an hour ago. Where are you?"

"Home."

"Get your carcass downtown, Counselor. Shake a leg."

"Soon, John. I've got company. There's a gentleman here I'd like you to meet. He's been tailing me about town. I decoyed him to my apartment and let him see my gun. He says he's a city detective and has a shield to prove it. I thought he might be working out of your office."

"What's his name?"

"Just a minute." I called to my visitor. "The lieutenant wants to know your name."

"Suchak—Gus Suchak. Detective second-grade."

The name rang a bell. And more, in fact. It struck a loud and resounding gong. I'd run across it twice before. Once on the list of men working with Sergeant Ernie Strobe the night Ben Keller was shelved. And again, as one of the birds questioned by Max Turner, the abusive one.

I relayed all this information to Nola.

His voice hardened. "I want him down here on the double.... Wait a minute. You'd better hold him. I'll be there in twenty minutes."

He broke the connection and I hung up.

Suchak was watching me in unblinking silence. His hands hung between his knees, the fingers slowly flexing. After a moment, he started to smile with a kind of cynical detachment. He put his hands on the arms of the chair and pushed himself upright.

"Sit down," I said sharply.

He shook his head. "Sorry. You're wasting the taxpayers' money. I'm getting back on the job."

He turned and strode deliberately toward the foyer.

The blue gabardine coat had a shine across the sloping shoulders. The dark homburg was planted squarely on his head. I had to admire the man's nerve, and my dilemma grew with each step he took. He was certain that I would not gun him down in cold blood. He would not credit me with the kind of pitiless brutality necessary to send a bullet crashing into another human being.

He was reaching for the doorknob when the .38 convulsed in my hand.

The explosion thundered in the confines of my living room and left my ears ringing. A slug bit viciously into the wall alongside Suchak's head. Fragments of plaster sprayed over his coat.

He spun around, slack-jawed with astonishment, his face washed of color. Mechanically, with no conscious volition, he slowly brushed the plaster from his sleeve and shoulder. Then he turned and stared stupidly at the punctured wall not ten inches from his right ear.

"It's your gun," I said. "You must have done some target shooting, so you know it's accurate. I'm a pretty fair marksman. That bullet went exactly where I wanted it to go. Next time I'll aim for your leg, just behind the knee."

"By God!" he said in a muffled voice. "I believe you're serious."

"Dead serious, Suchak. My secretary was murdered right where you're standing and I have a score to settle with somebody. Don't test me in my present frame of mind. Come back here and sit down." I raised my voice. "Come back here."

His eyes dueled with mine.

"Suchak," I said, "I'm going to stop you from walking out of here and maybe stop you from walking without a crutch for the rest of your life. For the last time, come back here."

He moved leadenly toward the chair, his eyes murky. He shrugged resignedly and sat down.

Not a word out of him now. He was lost in thought, the corners of his mouth pulled down. We did not have a long wait. Even in Manhattan a police car makes time. The bell rang and I stood to one side of the door for a moment. I would probably never use that peephole again. Then I opened up and admitted Nola.

He stepped briskly into the room. He ignored the gun in my hand and advanced toward Suchak. He planted himself solidly in front of the man and stared at him in stony-eyed silence.

"The name is Nola. Detective-lieutenant, Homicide. Did you ever hear of me?"

"Yes, sir."

"Stand up when you address a superior officer." His voice was a bark. "On your feet, mister."

Suchak lumbered out of the chair. His mouth was pinched and white. His neck was red.

"Let's see your shield."

Suchak produced it. Nola turned it over in his hand and tossed it back contemptuously.

"Where are you assigned?"

"The Rackets Squad."

So he's still working with Strobe, I thought.

"Jordan says you were following him. Why?"

Suchak smiled, if a mechanical distortion of the lips can be called a smile. "Jordan is mistaken, sir."

"What's that?"

"He's mistaken. I was not following him."

"Come off it, Suchak. I'm not here to listen to any vaudeville. I know Jordan. He's an old hand. He's been around. If he says you were tailing him, that's it."

"Sorry, Lieutenant. This time he's wrong."

"All right, Counselor," Nola said to me. "Let's have it in detail."

I recited. I told him how Suchak had stuck to me through a taxi ride and a winding promenade all the way to my apartment. And for a clincher I produced the list of names and held it up.

"Research," I said. "From a back copy of the *New*

York Times. A record of the men on duty with Strobe at the Crescent Hotel that night. Here he is, Gustaf Suchak, fourth from the top."

Nola's face turned to granite.

"The gentlemen are beginning to sweat," I said. "I wouldn't be surprised if one of them ambushed Max Turner this morning and put him in the hospital."

Nola's voice was tightly controlled. "Jordan made no mistake, Suchak. You were following him. Just remember, a woman was killed here last night. You're a police officer. If I find you guilty of suppressing evidence helpful to the solution of a homicide, I'll crack down. I'll haul you up on departmental charges. I'll put you behind bars. Do you read me, mister?"

Suchak's cheekbones were stained red in an otherwise gray face.

"I'm going to lay it out for you, mister. And then, by God, you're going to sound off. I'm not going to review the Keller incident. You've lived with it long enough. And so did an ex-colleague of yours, Fred Duncan. You sat on the truth, but he finally talked. He wrote a book and was murdered for his trouble. We're holding a client of Jordan's for the crime and Jordan's been chipping away at it ever since. He was threatened, he was warned to lay off. But he's not a man who scares easily. So there was an attempt on his life. It misfired and killed an innocent person. Two homicides, Suchak. Three if we count Keller. Any comment?"

A negative shake of the head.

"You say you're on the Rackets Squad. This happens to be high-class residential building. Just what the hell were you doing here?''

Moisture had formed along Suchak's lip. As a detective second-grade he rated a sergeant's pay. But there was a stain on his record from the Keller incident, and his rank was immutably set in cement. Suchak knew that. He knew, too, that he could ill afford to earn the enmity of a man like Nola. On the other hand, how could he admit complicity in past and recent events?

The gears and wheels were turning in his head. Then his face shifted subtly and he spoke in a quiet voice.

"I was not on duty today, Lieutenant. I was out for an airing when I spotted this character. . . . ''

"What character?''

"I'm not sure, sir. He seemed vaguely familiar. He resembled a man we'd shipped over some years ago for extortion. I didn't like the way he was acting. There was something peculiar about his movements. So I thought I'd tail him. And I was right behind him when he turned into this building.'' Suchak spread his palms. "What could I do? I followed him. I came into the lobby and was looking around when Jordan jumped me. I thought it was a holdup. So help me! I even offered him my money.''

I have always admired Nola's self-control. This time I didn't think he was going to make it. I watched him, holding my breath. Suddenly he wheeled toward the phone and began dialing with hard, angry movements. He waited impatiently, squeezing the instrument in his white-knuckled fist.

"Central Office Bureau,'' he grated when someone answered. "Hello. Get me Inspector Frank Connelly. Tell him Lieutenant John Nola, Homicide West wants him." There was a brief pause. "Hello, Frank. . . . Fine, fine, and you?" He literally pawed at the ground while amenities ate up time. "I need your help, Frank. I'm having a little trouble with one of your men. Gus Suchak. On the Rackets Squad, yes. I want you to call him in and hold him at Headquarters. I'll be down personally to explain. No, sir. He's here with me right now." Nola swiveled and extended the handset. "Inspector Connelly has some instructions for you."

Suchak walked heavily and took the phone gingerly. He cleared his throat. "Suchak speaking, Inspector." He listened, stolid and blank-faced, and hung up.

"You heard him," Nola said with acid precision. "Beat it. Get out of my sight."

Suchak started for the door, stiff-kneed.

"Wait a minute," I said. "You forgot your gun."

"Never mind," Nola rasped. "I'll deliver the piece downtown."

When he reached the door, Suchak closed it behind him softly and carefully as if it were made of very fragile glass.

Then the clutch slipped and I got a treat. In a tone of bottle fury Nola offered his opinion of Detective second-grade Gustaf Suchak. What rankled him most was the man's status as a cop. But his anger passed off quickly. He found one of his dappled cigars and clamped it between his teeth.

"What do you think?" I asked him.

"He's probably keeping an eye on you to see what progress you're making."

"Under Strobe's orders?"

"Probably. We'll check his gun, front and back. There may be a particle of skin from Turner's scalp on the butt. And we'll let Ballistics fire a test shell. We accomplished one thing, though."

"What's that?"

"We got him off your back. He knows he's suspect now and he'll have to keep his nose clean."

I smiled thinly. "And I thought maybe you had assigned him to protect me."

"This is a big city, Counselor. We have limited manpower. You'll have to protect yourself. And I suggest you start right away by seeing the District Attorney before he hauls you down in a paddy wagon."

24

"I'M JUST WAITING," Magowan said. He was in his office on the sixth floor of the Criminal Courts Building, wearing his official air of lofty censure.

"For what?" I asked.

"The first big slip. One of these days you'll step over the line and we'll squeeze the pliers good and hard. You've been a thorn in the chief's side for too long. He doesn't like you very much, Jordan."

"I'm sorry. Helping my clients is more important than winning a personality contest. Will it change things if I vote for him next year?"

"I'll ask. In the meantime he wants me to give you a message."

"Yes?"

"He's sorry about the death of your secretary. And he's worried about your reaction. He wants it clearly understood you're not to make this a personal vendetta. We've got a big unassimilated element in Manhattan now and a lot of tension. It's tough enough keeping the peace without an irresponsible lawyer on the warpath."

"I'll take it under advisement."

"You'll do more than that. You'll steer clear of this investigation. Punishment is not your province."

"Execution is not my province. Punishment is something else. Sorry, Magowan. I make no guarantees. You wouldn't want me to go through life with a frustration complex, would you?"

"Now listen, Jordan—"

"Don't worry," I said. "If I find him, you'll get him alive. Not healthy maybe, but alive."

He studied me for a moment, patently irritated. "Was Cassidy involved in anything? Did she have any enemies?"

"Why?"

"Why? The woman was murdered, that's why."

"I thought the D.A.'s office always cooperates with the police. Haven't you spoken to Lieutenant Nola?"

"And what is Lieutenant Nola's theory?"

"He claims her death was a mistake, the killer was after me."

"What do you claim?"

"I claim his point merits consideration. She was killed in my apartment through an aperture in a closed door, by someone who could not see or identify his victim. She was there at my request and no one knew about it."

"No one? Are you sure?"

And then I remembered. Barbara knew. Cassidy had answered when Barbara phoned. But I refused to read any significance into the fact.

"I'm sure," I lied. "Besides, my life had been threatened on the telephone earlier in the day."

He sat up. "By whom?"

"I don't know. I couldn't recognize the voice."

"You must have some suspicion."

"You're a prosecutor, Magowan. Suspicion is not proof."

"It can be used as a springboard for investigation."

"All right, then. You're holding Adam Coleman for the murder of Fred Duncan. On what motive? Presumably, a debt of two hundred thousand dollars. But you're overlooking an important fact. Duncan wrote a book exposing official corruption. If a movie were made, publicizing the facts, it would cause an uproar. And probably start a new investigation. Some of the people involved are still operating in their official capacity. They face exposure, condemnation, dismissal, and possible prosecution."

"I'm still listening."

"Isn't that enough? Good Lord, man, can't you see the seeds of violence sown in Duncan's book?"

"Certainly I see it. But you're forgetting one very important element."

"What's that?"

"Your client was found with Duncan's body, trying to get rid of it."

"No, sir. I'm not forgetting it. I say the body was planted in Coleman's car, a red herring to sidetrack the investigation. It also explains the attempt on my life."

"How?"

"Because I'm working for the truth."

"Then you think there's a connection between the two murders."

"Absolutely."

"Sounds a little farfetched to me."

"Look, Magowan. Two people are dead. On that score alone the theory ought to be worth testing.

And yet your office hasn't even asked for a copy of Duncan's book. Why? What are you afraid of?''

''I assume you're making a point.''

''Damn right I am. A detail from this office was responsible for Ben Keller's safety. He was your star witness. You had a chance to rid the community of a deadly blight, and that chance went out the window with Keller. Are you afraid it will show the D.A. in a bad light?''

''This office had no control over the situation, Jordan, and you know it. We can't be blamed for Keller's death.''

''Perhaps not. But how about the feeble and half-hearted investigation that followed? And the official report. Suicide.'' I gave a snort of disgust. ''That was whitewash, Magowan.''

He had no comment, looking sour.

''What are you worried about?'' I said. ''The incident took place under a different administration. Your boss wasn't even District Attorney at the time. Even at this late date a vigorous investigation would go far in restoring confidence and prestige to the prosecutor's office.''

''That would suit your purpose fine, wouldn't it?''

''I don't deny that. Naturally your help would be welcome. You have the men, the money, the facilities, and if—''

His phone rang and he unbent his elbow. He listened briefly and said, ''Yes, sir. I'll be right in.'' He stood up. ''Sorry, Jordan. The chief wants me. Just remember what I said.'' We left his office together.

I debated whether or not to visit Adam while I was there. Then I remembered my untended office and decided against it. Something would have to be done about getting at least a temporary replacement for Cassidy. I stopped off at the lobby to phone an employment agency and ask for applicants.

All afternoon the foot traffic was heavy, a steady procession of candidates. It was a distressing and repugnant chore. And discouraging. Cassidy could be replaced but never duplicated.

Scenically, most of the prospects held up rather well. They came in various heights and the usual shapes, with hair that ran the full color spectrum. Several possessed adequate legal training but were rejected on other grounds.

One kept her jaws working incessantly on a wad of gum. Another appeared with a neckline low enough to make any male client forget why he'd come to see me. The voice of a third had strident and disconcerting overtones. A fourth was so proud of her teeth she wore a perpetual smile. And so it went, and I was almost ready to concede defeat, even though it meant being snowed under, when Hildy Carter walked into the office.

"How do you do," she said in a nicely modulated voice, with no regional characteristics. "The Brooks Agency sent me."

I sat up and took notice.

Her manner was impersonal but direct. She had composure and a quiet look of confidence. Her tailored suit was neither prim nor specially designed to accentuate components. There was a minimum amount of makeup on her face, which indeed needed none.

I glanced at the agency card and saw that she had worked two years for Casement, Kahn, Solomon &

Proxmire, an overstuffed and prosperous outfit specializing in insurance law.

"Sit down, Miss Carter," I said.

Her posture was straight but not strained.

"Why did you leave Casement, Kahn and so forth?"

"One of the partners forgot that I was an employee."

"I see. How's your shorthand?"

"Would you care to dictate a letter?"

I handed her a steno pad and fired off a rapid volley. "Type that, please. The machine at the reception desk."

I listened to the clatter, and her speed, while unexceptional, was adequate. She returned with the sample. Spelling and punctuation were perfect. No errors in content.

"What made you become a legal secretary, Miss Carter?"

"My father was a lawyer. I used to work for him during vacations."

"Would I recogonize his name?"

"Probably not. He practiced upstate, in Goshen."

"Then I take it you're well acquainted with legal forms."

"Sufficiently, I believe."

"Do you know what an examination in supplementary proceedings is?"

"Yes. An attempt to find property that may be levied on to satisfy a judgment."

"How about certiorari?"

"That's a writ requiring some lower court to relinquish a proceeding or the records involved." She saw my expression and smiled modestly. "I studied law for a while, but gave it up when my father died."

"Do you know what happened to my secretary?" I asked.

"Yes. It's in all the papers."

"And you have no misgivings or reservations about this job?"

"No, sir."

"Do you mind working late on occasion?"

"That depends on the frequency and the salary."

"I can't guarantee the first, but the second will be adequate. Would you like this job?"

"Suppose we try each other for a month or so."

"When can you start?"

"When do you need me?"

"Right now, Miss Carter. Immediately."

"I'm ready," she said.

Finding someone who knew the ropes and could make a decision was almost too good to be true.

"For this afternoon," I said, "you have three projects. Answer the phone, keep the journalists off my neck, and familiarize yourself with the files. Two cases particularly, *Duncan* v. *Coleman*, and a probate matter involving the estate of M. Parker Coleman. Let me brief you on the relationships involved."

She listened attentively, absorbing facts, with an occasional pertinent question. The phone rang and she reached for it automatically.

"Scott Jordan's office. Who's calling, please. I'm sorry, sir. He's not available at the moment." She hung up.

I lifted a questioning eyebrow at her.

"Somebody from the *News*," she said.

We heard the outer door open. She rose quickly

and went into the reception room. A moment later she reappeared carrying a document.

It was a motion to amend the title *Fred Duncan* v. *Adam Coleman* because of the plaintiff's death. The phone rang again and Hildy Carter took it. She looked up at me and said, "Mr. Gil Dodd."

I nodded and reached for the instrument.

"No success," he reported. "I called the hotel managers and asked them to check their safes. None of them found the old man's will or papers belonging to him of any kind."

"Well, it was a possibility we had to check. How were things at Adam's office?"

"Lot of mail. Nothing important. I'll take care of it this afternoon."

"Did you find a copy of Duncan's manuscript?"

He uttered a regretful exclamation. "I forgot to look. I'll check it again tomorrow."

While we were talking, someone had entered the reception room. Now Hildy Carter came back with another paper. She waited for me to hang up, then placed it on my desk, her face impassive.

It was a notice from the Bar Association, directing me to appear before the Executive Committee for a special hearing next Wednesday on the complaint of Mrs. Lorraine Coleman.

I deflated instantly. All my rhetoric had been useless. Alfred Seward had not been impressed. And now, in addition to everything else, I would have to marshal some kind of defense. It was a serious charge and I felt like a long-tailed cat in a room full of rockers.

I sat for a moment, gloomy and thoughtful. Then I stood up and said, "Mind the store, Miss Carter. I'm going over to the Merchant's Trust."

25

Mr. William Chalker was one of five executives, all seated behind a line of rosewood desks along one side of the bank. His polished shoes rested on beige-colored broadloom. He was a bland, portly gent, conservatively dressed in a sober suit. He had a clerical face and steel-rimmed glasses.

He peered down at my card and then up at me with cautiously heightened interest.

"Scott Jordan. I read about you in the papers. Aren't you the attorney for Adam Coleman?"

"That's right."

"His father was one of our most valued customers. Gave us quite a jolt here at the bank when they accused young Adam of killing our vault attendant." He shook his head incredulously. "Still can't believe it."

"Your instincts are sounder than the District Attorney's. Adam will be exonerated."

"I hope so. Seemed like such a nice chap. And old Fred," he added, marveling, "writing a book in his spare time and selling it to the movies. Never thought he had it in him. Dour sort of beggar, but a mighty efficient custodian." Sunlight pushed through the vast window front and glinted on his spectacles. "What can I do for you, Mr. Jordan?"

"I need some information."

"Yes?"

"Concerning the account of M. Parker Coleman."

"You understand, of course, Mr. Jordan, that banks seldom disclose the affairs of their clients, living or dead, to anyone. Except," he added with a wry twist of his mouth, "to government officials, when necessary."

"Naturally. A wise and prudent policy. Which I respect. But the information I want breaches no trust and violates no confidence. Of course, I would expect you to be the exclusive judge of that."

"Of course."

I said, "I know that Mr. Coleman retired some years ago and traveled extensively. He was a wealthy man with a substantial portfolio of securities that needed constant attention. Interest, dividends, subscription rights, that sort of thing. A custodial account here at the bank would have been a great convenience, with you people keeping all the records and merely crediting his account with income."

"A great convenience," he echoed.

"Did he have such an account?"

"Why do you ask?"

"Because he left a large estate and I represent his children. We know that he drew a last will and testament, but so far no trace of the document has been found."

"Most odd, Mr. Jordan. Men of means are generally scrupulous in guarding their important papers."

"Exactly. And it occurred to me that if he had a custodial account, it might be in the bank's private vaults with his other papers."

Mr. Chalker shook his head. "I'm afraid not. Securities, bonds, deeds—yes. But not a will unless he named the bank as his executor."

"Which he did not do,"

"Not to my knowledge. Have you searched his safe-deposit box?"

"The widow did, yes."

"And it is not there."

"No, sir."

"Then I don't see how I can be of any help, Mr. Jordan."

"It would help us to know the last time he had access to his box. There is always a chance that he withdrew the will himself and destroyed it."

Mr. Chalker was frowning uncertainly. "Well, now, I—"

"Surely no one would object to this information. His heirs have a right to know, and as their attorney I have that right, too. What's more, we're legally obligated to exhaust every possibility in trying to locate a will. And I believe the bank is obliged to help us. Certainly, if Mr. Coleman were alive, he would not object. We merely want to ascertain the facts."

Mr. Chalker wavered perceptibly. He considered it and found no violation of the bank's ethics. "That is all you want to know, when Mr. Coleman last visited his box?"

"Yes."

He sighed deeply and reached for the phone. He got through to the proper extension and issued instructions. Then he hung up and tapped his fingers on the glass top of his desk. After a moment he removed the steel-rimmed spectables and wiped them carefully with a spotless handkerchief.

It was closing time and they were letting no more customers through the front door. The tellers were beginning to check their accounts. A messenger arrived with a slip of paper. Mr. Chalker took it and thanked him. He examined the notation and said, "Ah, here it is. M. Parker Coleman visited his safe-deposit box on the fourteenth of this month."

I stared at him. Blinking. And then expelled one astonished word.

"*What!*"

Mr. Chalker was taken aback. The unexpected volume and force of my voice had startled him. He swallowed apprehensively and shrank into his chair.

"The fourteenth of this month?" I demanded, slow and deliberate.

"Er...yes, that's what it says."

"Impossible." Flat and emphatic.

"I...I beg your pardon, sir."

"The fourteenth of this month was a week ago. A week ago Mr. M. Parker Coleman was in St. John's Hospital, suffering a severe coronary occlusion, flat on his back, under oxygen and completely immobilized."

William Chalker turned pale. Sudden anxiety wrenched at his face. He shook his head, stammering. "There must...there must be some mistake."

"There is, Mr. Chalker. There certainly is. A very grave mistake. Made by the Merchant's Trust."

"How so?"

"Somebody else apparently got into Mr. Coleman's safe-deposit box. Now how in the royal name of hell could a stranger do that?"

"He couldn't. I assure you, Mr. Jordan, it's a physical impossibility. We have a foolproof system

here. Our safe-deposit boxes are absolutely inviolable."

"Not if somebody else signed Mr. Coleman's signature and was given access. May I see that piece of
paper?"

He hugged it protectively to his chest, "Oh, no.
No, sir. I'm afraid not. This slip of paper is the property of the bank, part of its confidential records."

"Nonsense. It can be subpoenaed by court action."

"That may be, sir. I don't know. I'm not a lawyer.
But it's a step you would have to take before we
relinquish it."

I relaxed and smiled amiably. "Come now, Mr.
Chalker. This is a friendly discussion. There's no
reason to get upset. I'm sure you can find some
logical explanation. I have only one request. Take
care of that slip of paper. Keep it in a safe place. I
wouldn't want it to get lost or mislaid."

He looked hurt. "This is a bank, Mr. Jordan. We
are most zealous in guarding our records."

"I'm delighted to hear it. One more question, if I
may, sir. You say there is no way for an unauthorized
stranger to get his hands into another man's safe-
deposit box?"

"None whatever." He was growing a bit waspish.
"It's unheard of. The Merchant's Trust has installed
the most modern equipment and we employ every
possible safeguard."

"You're certain?"

"Positive." His chubby fist landed emphatically
on the desk. "Unconditionally and unequivocally
positive."

I shook my head. "It seems to me that I recollect a

few decisions where depositors won sizable judg-
ments for boxes that were violated and looted.''

"In the past, perhaps. Not recently.''

"I'll check into it.''

His manner was hardening with hostility and he
sat, holding his lips prim.

"Would you tell me this?" I asked. "Who was the
custodian on duty that day?''

But there were no further disclosures from Mr.
William Chalker. He squared his shoulders resolutely. "I'm afraid that will be all for today, Mr. Jordan.
I'm sorry. I just can't spare any more time. Now, if
you will excuse me. . . .''

"Sure," I said. "I understand. There may be
evidence of laxity or dereliction and the bank wants
to cover itself. A conference with other officials is
called for. Please remember what I told you about
that slip of paper. And thank you for your time and
trouble. Good day, sir.''

I left; harried lines were deepening on the ordinarily placid face.

26

THE HUMAN ANTHROPOID is an acquisitive organism. Much of his brief span is devoted to harvesting wealth and squirreling it away.

He is also ingenious.

To safeguard his valuables he has devised the highly complicated bank vault. Its great builders in this country are Mosler and York. Behind Gibraltar-like concrete, their steel-encased fortresses, guarded by multiple time locks and ear-splitting burglar alarms, are extremely efficient, immune to the acetylene torch or nitroglycerin.

Immune to everything, perhaps, except a nuclear explosion, and if it came to that, what good would a pulverized tiara be to an atomized dowager?

Still, the fact remained—someone had breached the vault at the Merchant's Trust.

If I could prove this, I had my defense for the Grievance Committee of the Bar Association. And the man to help me was Mr. Harvey Hecht, a vice-president of the Safe Deposit Association.

I found him in his office on Park Avenue, a compact gentleman with a military carriage and a head of prematurely white, brush-cut hair. Some years ago I had represented him in a negligence suit and he was duly grateful for a sizable recovery.

He welcomed me with a warm smile.

The smiled faded when I told him what I wanted.

He sat behind his desk and studied me with long-faced deliberation. "Let me get this straight, Counselor. You want to know if it's possible for a stranger to gain access to another man's safe-deposit box, is that it?"

"Not *if*," I said. "*How?*"

"Are you involved in such a case?"

"Yes."

He stroked his jaw. "It's a subject we don't like to discuss around here."

"Naturally. I figured you'd be sensitive and touchy about it, but I seem to recall several cases that reached court and they're all a matter of public record. I haven't got the time to chase them down and I'd appreciate your help."

He pinched his bottom lip, deliberating for a moment. Then he sighed and said, "Do you remember the Bechtel case?"

"Not offhand."

"Happened 'way back in 1947. The victim was a bank right here in New York. Mrs. Bechtel had sold a business which she'd inherited. She put the money into her safe-deposit box, and then, some months later, she returned to the bank and opened her box. Ten thousand was missing. Or so she claimed. Naturally, she sued the bank. The case took seven years."

"And the outcome?"

"It developed that safe-deposit boxes were not entirely foolproof. A lot of bank officials got ulcers from the testimony that emerged."

"Would you elaborate?"

The tiniest and most pusillanimous smile touched his lips.

"There are two keys to every box, as you probably know. The customer's key and the guard key retained by the bank. This is an excellent idea, except for one weakness. The human element involved. Naturally, we have to employ custodians. And the strength of our whole system depends upon their reliability."

"How?"

"It is possible for a larcenous custodian to make a wax impression of the customer's key. He could then loot the box at his leisure."

"Is there no solution?"

"A partial one. The rules now compel a customer to keep his own key in his own possession at all times."

"Why partial?"

"Because of the Bechtel case. You know what her lawyer proved? He brought a locksmith to court and put him on the witness stand. The man demonstrated that with the compartment door open, three small screws are exposed. In thirty seconds he could whip out the lock and install a doctored lock in its place."

"I see. And that would give him access any time he wanted it."

"Yes. Provided he had the manual dexterity and was so inclined."

"Well, now," I said. "My bank leaves the compartment door open after I've taken the box out to check the contents. Why don't they keep it locked?"

He made a vinegar mouth.

"They used to. And that was no good, either. Let

me tell you what happened in one instance. While the custodian was busy elsewhere, some felonious customer walked out with a box concealed under his coat. The custodian forgot all about him. A couple of weeks later, he returned. When they opened his compartment, no box. He let out a howl and acted frantic. He screamed that he'd been robbed.''

"Ingenious," I said.

"Sure." He looked sour. "But we couldn't prove it. And the bank had to make good. Leave the compartment door open or keep it locked. What's the solution? It's six of one and half a dozen of the other. We can't win.''

Harvey Hecht leaned back, a jaundiced and disillusioned man, contemplating the vagaries of human behavior.

"You have your problems," I said.

"And they never end. Want to hear more?"

"Yes.''

"There was a small upstate bank with a crooked custodian. The custodian had a friend who rented a box. As a customer the friend was given a key. He had a duplicate made. And later he surrendered the box. He gave the duplicate to the custodian. In due time, the box was rented again.''

"Hah!" I said. "The new customer had as much safety as if he'd left his valuables in a cafeteria restroom.''

Hecht nodded gloomily. "That's about the size of it.''

"Why don't they scramble the locks—change them every time a box is surrendered?"

"Sometimes we do, Jordan. But it doesn't solve the problem.''

"Why not?"

"Because the manufacturer stamps a code number on each lock and these codes are common knowledge to locksmiths throughout the country."

"So all a dishonest custodian needs is to spot the code number for his particular duplicate key and he's in."

"That's right."

"My God!" I said. "Is there no solution at all?"

"We're trying all the time, Jordan. Right now, we're working on a tight system of key control. Dual supervision by two people at all times. A choice for the customer of several keys in sealed envelopes. Strict enforcement governing admission to the vaults. And, of course, a more reliable identification system."

"Will all that make it absolutely foolproof?"

"The only foolproof system, Counselor, is a loyal and trustworthy employee."

"I believe the commodity exists."

"I hope so. If it doesn't, then we're doomed." He pushed his chair back. "I hope I've been instructive—or at least interesting."

"You've been both. I'm greatly indebted."

"Demonstrate it by not suing any of our member banks."

I smiled. Harvey Hecht smiled. We shook hands and he took me to the door. The elevator was crowded with people leaving for the day. Downstairs, the streets seethed as the massive concrete honeycombs yielded their workers. Frayed humanity clustered at bus stops and converged on subway kiosks.

The sun had retreated beyond the Hudson, leaving a chill in the air. Watching the homeward-bound horde I felt a vague stirring of envy. Nothing for them to worry about until tomorrow. A whole evening of relaxation. Dinner and a comfortable chair in front of the television set. Nothing to do but sit, benumbed and hypnotized by assorted comics, cowboys, and private eyes performing their antics in the great anodyne of forgetfulness.

I stopped off at a telephone booth and called the office.

For a moment I thought I had the wrong number. Over the years I had gotten used to Cassidy's voice answering that particular combination of digits. And then I remembered my new secretary, Hildy Carter.

"Still there?" I asked, glancing at my watch.

"Yes, Mr. Jordan. I was waiting for your call. I stayed because you have visitors."

"Who?"

"A woman, Mrs. Ruth Duncan, and a little boy. She came without an appointment and insisted on waiting."

"I'll be right over," I said. "You can leave when you want to."

"And there's a message, Mr. Jordan. Miss Barbara Coleman phoned. She'll be working late at the LeMar Studios and will you pick her up there when you're free."

"All right," I said and hung up.

Traffic was too heavy for a cab, so I stretched my legs, hurrying toward the office.

27

HILDY CARTER WAS WAITING for me in the reception room.

"They're inside," she said, nodding toward my office.

I took out my keys, disconnected one and handed it to her. "I don't know when I'll be in tomorrow. Open up about nine."

"Of course. Will there be anything else?"

"Not today. You can leave now."

She was tidying her desk when I walked into my office.

Ruth Duncan looked up from the client's chair where she sat, patiently clasping her purse. Peter was standing at the window, wide-eyed, awed by the panorama below. On the ice-skating rink in the plaza, whirling figures cut intricate patterns, and around them silhouetted buildings stretched into the sky. Peter turned shyly at my entrance.

"How do you do, Peter," I said. "Good to see you again."

He was dressed for the occasion, wearing a suit and striped tie, knotted slightly off center. He took my proffered hand with an air of grave dignity.

"Peter," his mother reminded him gently.

"Thank you for the candy," he said.

"You're quite welcome."

"I have one piece after lunch and one piece after supper. Linda, too."

"I left Linda with a neighbor," Ruth Duncan explained. "I wanted Peter to tell you something."

I looked at him with interest.

"He's an imaginative boy," she said, "but he never makes up stories. It's something he heard. Something his grandfather said. I'm not sure if it means anything but it may be helpful." She turned and smiled at him encouragingly. "Peter, you remember that last evening you were playing with grandpa?"

"Uh-huh."

"Would you tell Mr. Jordan what happened?"

The large solemn eyes met mine. "Grandpa didn't stay long. He had to leave. He was going to see his daddy."

I frowned and glanced at Ruth Duncan. She shrugged helplessly, looking bewildered.

"Well, now, Peter," I said. "Did grandpa tell you he was going to see his daddy?"

"No. But he spoke to him on the telephone."

"You heard him?"

"Yes. We were playing with my coloring set and grandpa kept looking at his watch. Then he said he had to call somebody and he went to the telephone and took a piece of paper out of his pocket and he dialed a number."

"You told me you want to be a policeman, Peter, didn't you?"

"Yes."

"Well, policemen have to remember things. Try

hard, Peter, and see if you can remember everything grandpa said.''

He looked intent and very serious. His thin face squinched up in an agony of concentration.

''Did he say hello?'' I prompted.

''Everybody says hello on the telephone.''

''And what did he say next?''

''Well, I don't remember the zact words. Grandpa spoke a little funny, you know.''

''Try, Peter. As near as you can remember.''

He fidgeted, scuffing a shoe at the leg of a chair. ''Grandpa told his daddy he had to see him, it was important. And then he said, 'All right, I'll be there.'''

''Did he say where, Peter?''

''I don't remember.''

''And then what happened?''

''Then he hung up.''

''Did he leave right away?''

''No,'' Ruth Duncan volunteered. ''He wouldn't leave Peter alone. He waited until I came back and then he said he had to get washed and change his clothes.''

I felt a surge of excitement, an acceleration of my pulse. But I kept my voice level and my face blank and I looked at Ruth Duncan. ''Where did Fred live?''

''Three blocks from where I do.'' She gave me an address.

''Do you have a key?''

''Oh, yes. I used to go there several times a week to tidy up.''

''Would you mind if I had a look at the place?''

''Not at all.'' She opened her purse and began rummaging. She found a key and held it out.

I was writing Duncan's address on a piece of paper when the phone rang and I picked it up.

"Mr. Jordan?" The voice was breathless.

"Speaking."

"This is Mrs. Wallace—Lorna Wallace, remember?"

"Of course. Kate's mother."

"Yes. I promised to call you if I heard from Kate. Well, I got a telegram just a little while ago. Kate says she's fine and I'm not to worry and she's writing me a long letter to tell me all about it."

"That's fine, Mrs. Wallace. I said you'd hear from her."

"Yes you did. And you were right."

"Where did the wire originate from, Mrs. Wallace?"

"I beg your pardon."

"Where is Kate now."

"Oh! Just a moment." I could hear the faint rustle of paper and then her voice again. "Kate's in Mexico. . .Acapulco." She paused. "I hope I'm doing the right thing. Nothing's going to happen to Kate, is it, Mr. Jordan?"

Kate would suffer a little. That couldn't be helped. But the human spirit is resilient and a broken heart readily heals.

"Kate's going to be fine," I said. "You did the right thing, Mrs. Wallace. And thank you for calling." We hung up.

So Dan Varney was in Mexico.

No wonder Max Turner had found no record of any passport. None is needed to cross the border.

I felt that familiar sense of excitement, the visceral tremor, the sudden tension. I was approaching a precipice in uncharted territory, and over its edge were revelations that could break this case wide open. Already it was straining at the seams.

I thanked Ruth Duncan and shook hands soberly with Peter. I took them down to the street and put them in a cab and gave the driver a bill. Then I went back to the office and went to work on the telephone. I got through to Max Turner at the hospital.

He was irritated and resentful at his enforced confinement. "How do you feel, Max?" I asked him.

"Well enough," he grumbled. "Except for a headache. If I could find my clothes I'd sneak out of here."

"They're discharging you tomorrow. Think you can travel?"

"Sure. Where?"

"Mexico."

"Well, now. Mexico. What's up, Counselor?"

"There a good chance we've located Varney. I think he's holed up in Acapulco. I want you to fly down there first thing in the morning."

"And if I find him?"

"Let me know at once. I'll start the wheels rolling on extradition proceedings at this end. Have you got that?"

"Yes, sir."

"I'll call Aeromexico and make a reservation. A ticket will be waiting for you at Kennedy. I'll have them notify you of the exact time and flight number."

"They can reach me here all night."

"Take care, Max. And don't stop any bullets."

I hung up and reached for the telephone directory. I found the LeMar Studios and dialed their number. They were still working, a voice told me, and Barbara Coleman was on camera at the moment, would I care to wait. I said no, and please give her a message—Mr. Jordan would pick her up there within the hour.

I left the office and headed uptown.

Fred Duncan had lived in a modest walk-up on the third floor. The key Ruth Duncan had given me opened his door. Naturally, the police had been there before me. But they were shooting in the dark, not sure what to look for.

Duncan, apparently, had been a neat, methodical man. No clothes were strewn haphazardly about. So I checked the garments in his closet. In a pair of serge trousers I found a penknife, a cigar trimmer, a clipping from one of the newspapers about Zenith Films' tentative plans for the casting of *The Kingpins* and a sip of paper with two telephone numbers—555-0010 and 555-8624. The first looked vaguely familiar, the second I recognized at once.

It was my own.

The room was close and musty. I opened one of the windows and sat on a hard-backed chair to concentrate. The naked globe overhead cast its niggardly illumination over a round cloth-covered table. Ideas digested in my head, disconnected theories. I nourished them with fresh revelations, and out of the jigsaw a picture began to focus. A picture I did not like. And I liked it even less on closer inspection.

The LeMar Studios were located in a barnlike structure converted from an old carriage house. They were still working. Barbara, caparisoned in yards of textured silk, sat on a stone bench in front of an ancient Greek column. A battery of floodlights glared down at her mercilessly. A slight chap flitted about her with hummingbird gestures, tilting her chin at various angles and backing off to survey the effect.

"That's it, darling," he suddenly chirped. "Hold it now."

He pranced behind his camera and got under the hood. An assistant held the tripping mechanism high in his hand. When he got the signal he triumphantly clicked the button.

The little man emerged from under the hood, beaming. "You were fine, Barbi, fine. I guess that's it for today."

She got up, stretched, saw me waiting, and came over, greeting me with both hands. "What an afternoon! Four straight hours of posing. I'm dead."

"You need a drink."

"Yes, doctor. I'll get it at Vickie's. We're invited there for dinner. What time is it?"

I glanced at my watch and told her.

"We can just make it. Let me get out of this costume and I'll join you in a moment."

28

THE NIGHT had turned murky. Clouds moved in, darkening the sky. There was moisture in the air. And electricity. A deep-throated ominous rumble of thunder brought Barbara closer to my side in the cab.

By the time we got out, it was raining.

Victoria opened the door. "I was getting worried. Come on in."

She took our coats.

Gil Dodd was at the cellaret, mixing martinis. Apparently he'd been testing the concoction. There was a rosy flush to his square brown face. He filled some glasses and dropped in a twist of lemon peel.

Victoria refused a drink. She wanted an immediate council of war, asking about Adam.

"He's bearing up," I told her.

"Do they treat him decently?"

"Well, it's not the Waldorf. Neither is it a concentration camp."

"How about bail?"

"I spoke to the District Attorney. He refused to cooperate. But the picture isn't all black. There's good news, too."

Barbara stirred, suddenly alert. "Well, tell us."

"I think we've found Dan Varney."

Questions flew. They all jabbered simultaneously. I told them about Kate Wallace, and about my up-state visit to her mother. I told them about the tele-gram and my assumption that Kate had gone to join Varney in Mexico.

"What do we do now?" Barbara demanded.

"It's already done," I said. "I have a man flying down there tomorrow morning. We'll haul Varney back on extradition proceedings. I doubt if he's spent too much of that two hundred thousand dollars. We're nailing him too soon. So most of the loot will be recovered. Enough, anyway to clean up the Duncan lawsuit."

Barbara clapped her hands rhapsodically.

Gil Dodd glowed. "That's capital news. I'm de-lighted, Jordan."

But Victoria brought them down to earth. "What are we crowing about? It doesn't help Adam on that murder charge, does it?"

"No," I said. "But there's other evidence piling up all the time. New elements have come to light. I think we can offer the District Attorney a much bet-ter candidate than Adam."

"Who?" demanded Dodd. "That police sergeant? Ernie Strobe?"

I shook my head. "Not him."

"Well, who then?" Barbara's voice rose impa-tiently.

"The same person who shot Cassidy."

"But I thought you were sure Strobe did it, that he meant you to be the victim, that he shot Cassidy by mistake."

"The mistake was mine," I said. "I was never the

intended victim. That bullet was meant for Cassidy and she died as planned.''

Victoria was frowning. ''I don't understand. An ordinary secretary. What possible motive could anyone have?''

''Far from ordinary,'' I said. ''And the motive was substantial. Close to one million dollars.''

Three pairs of eyes stared at me in silence. Then Gil Dodd gave a short, skeptical laugh.

''You mean Cassidy had a million dollars?''

''No. But she was the key that meant a million dollars to someone else.''

''How do you mean?'' Barbara asked quietly.

''It all turned on your father's will. Oliver Wendell Rogers drew the document. Cassidy was his secretary and she typed it. So she knew what it said and could testify to its contents. I told you that a missing will could be probated by the testimony of two witnesses.''

''Of course. Rogers was one and Cassidy would be the other.''

''Correct. But the law makes a further provision. A correct copy can replace one of the witnesses. So in order to nullify your father's will, to prevent its probate under any circumstances, two measures were essential. All copies had to be destroyed and one of the witnesses had to be killed.''

A faint tremor ran through Victoria's long, austere body and she stood watching me in a kind of hypnotic trance.

Barbara had grown a little formal. ''There's an unpleasant implication here, Scott. You say Cassidy was murdered to prevent the probate of dad's will.''

''Correct.''

"But only his children would benefit by that—Adam and Vickie and me."

"That's right." I met her lofty stare without budging.

"And you say Adam is innocent. That leaves only Vickie and me. Which one of us are you accusing?"

Gil Dodd tried to break the tension with a feeble laugh. "Come now, Barbara. He doesn't mean anything of the kind."

She ignored him. "I want an answer, Scott."

"And you're entitled to one. But it needs a little background. Please indulge me." I drew a long breath. "You all know about an ex-cop, Fred Duncan, who desperately needed money. Fortunately—or unfortunately, depending on your point of view—he knew of a way to get it. He had information that would make a fascinating story. So he wrote a book. For a nonprofessional it must have been a backbreaking chore. But there were obstacles and Duncan was a practical man. He realized it would be suicide to market the book while Albert Jaekel was alive. So he waited. And in due time, Jaekel, who lived by violence, died by violence. With the danger gone, Duncan took his manuscript to Adam. And a movie sale was made which exceeded his wildest expectations. Two hundred thousand dollars would fulfill a dream to make a better life for his two grandchildren.

"And then disaster struck. Dan Varney absconded with the money. You can imagine Duncan's reaction. Frenzied and desperate, he went to a lawyer. The lawyer told him that Adam, as Varney's partner, was legally responsible and would have to make good. So there was a ray of light and he sued. Only to face another disappointment. Adam was broke, unable to satisfy a judgment of two hundred thousand dollars if Duncan won.''

"We know all this," Dodd said. "I don't see—"

"You will." I held up my hand. "Let me get on with it. So here was Duncan, facing defeat even if he won. But suddenly the picture brightened. Along came someone with a solution to his problem. Adam needed money to cover the debt. Duncan could help him get that money.''

"How?" Barbara demanded.

"Easy. Adam's father was dying. He would leave a large estate. By the terms of his will, Adam got nothing. If he died without a will, Adam would inherit close to a million dollars. But a will did exist. And it was locked away in your father's safe-deposit box. That will had to be removed and destroyed.''

Barbara shook her head. "I don't understand. It isn't possible to rob a man's safe-deposit box.''

"You're wrong," I said. "It not only is possible, but it has been done. And it was done to your father. The records at his bank show that he went to his box only a week ago.''

It took a moment to register and then she blurted, "But dad was in the hospital then.''

"Precisely.''

She was staring at me, lips parted. Victoria, fists clenched at her sides, looked ill. Dodd threw his hands out.

"Good Lord! I'm an accountant. I never heard of such a thing.''

"All it needed," I said, "was a duplicate key and the cooperation of the custodian. He would accept a forged signature slip and open the box. Duncan may have had scruples. I don't know. If he did, they were easily overcome."

"But the key. How could anyone get possession of a man's key?"

"Would that be so difficult? Where does a man generally keep his safe-deposit key? In a desk at his office or a chest at home. Available to a business associate or any member of his family who suspected that it might come in handy some day. You, for example, Dodd. You, as chief auditor of the chain, might have picked up that key and struck a duplicate."

Victoria managed to speak. Her voice was harsh and strangled. "Is this the man we hired as our lawyer? I think he's a little insane. Do we have to listen to him?"

I felt sorry for her. But not sorry enough to back down.

"There's insanity here all right," I said. "On Duncan's part for accepting the proposition. For thinking he could pull it off safely. For not destroying the record of that visit to the bank. Habit, I suppose, prevailed. He followed the same procedure he'd used hundreds of times in the past. He filed the signature slip along with the others."

Victoria said grittily. "I don't believe it."

"That may be. Nevertheless it exists and is available. Proof that the box was opened and the will destroyed. But the conspirators were not yet clear. A copy of the will was on file in my office. And that copy, if corroborated by only one witness, would admit the will to probate. So it, too, had to be destroyed. Cassidy was lured out of the office and the copy stolen. Now no documentary trace existed."

"Then why kill Cassidy?" Barbara asked.

"Because there were two witnesses alive who could testify to the will's provisions. Rogers, who was unavailable, and Cassidy, who was here in New York."

There were wrinkles in Barbara's brow. "If Duncan was so cooperative, why did he have to die, too?"

"Because he posed a constant threat of exposure. Then, too, he might become unmanageable after Cassidy was murdered. Robbing a safe-deposit box was one thing. Murder was something else. His reaction when that happened could not be assessed. And I suspect he made demands. Maybe he wanted a substantial donation at once. No. Duncan had served his purpose. Alive, he was trouble. Dead, he would never be a problem."

"But why in Adam's car?"

"Why not? He could be lured there easily enough. And it would mislead the police. Adam was having trouble with Duncan on an entirely different matter, unrelated to the will. He was a perfect patsy. It would take the heat off the real killer. And it served another purpose. Suppose Adam was convicted. It would throw his inheritance into the pot, increasing the share of the survivors. So he was framed. And to keep him from disposing of the body, one of the tires on his car was deflated. The trap was sprung when Adam tried to drive away."

Barbara's nostrils had flared. "That's fiendish! Utterly fiendish! Framing Adam to inherit more money. Dear God! He's my brother. He might have been convicted and sent away for life. How could you suggest such a thing—from me or Vickie?"

She appealed to her sister. Victoria stood mute, her throat constricted, incapable of speech. She knew the truth. It had been growing in her for some time, a malignant cancer, poisoning her soul. She averted her eyes, shaking her head negatively from side to side.

"Not you," I said. "And not Vickie. Someone else stood to gain. Someone not especially concerned about Adam. They were not related, except by marriage." I turned and looked at him. "How about it, Dodd?"

His fingers spread wide across his chest, but his laugh had a hollow ring. "Me? Are you accusing me?" The shock in his voice was fraudulent.

"Yes," I said. "I'm accusing you of two brutal and cold-blooded murders."

"My wife is right. The man's insane. How could I know that Cassidy would be in your apartment that night?"

"You knew. Barbara called my number from here and you heard her. You listened. You knew she was meeting me for dinner. It was an opportunity that called for immediate action and you took it. You expected me to be gone when you got there. And when you saw that look-through hole in the door you improvised. It made her death seem like a monstrous mistake, in no way linked to the Coleman estate."

"Pure assumption. Fantasy."

"Is it? Your wife knows you went out that night. Look at her." Despair had squeezed Victoria's face into a wretched mask. "And I know that Duncan called you and made an appointment the night he was killed."

"Proof, Jordan. Have you any proof?"

"Yes. Duncan's grandson was there at the time and he heard the man speak your name. *Dodd,* he said. And repeated it. But Duncan had a Scottish accent and the boy made a mistake. He thought Duncan was saying *dad,* talking to his father."

"You call that proof?" Sarcasm laced his voice. "The mistake of a three-and-a-half-year-old boy?"

"And how would you know the boy's age?" I said. "Or anything else about Duncan's family if you hadn't investigated? No, sir. My proof goes deeper. Duncan had your number on a piece of paper— 555-0010, in his own handwriting. I found it in the suit he was wearing that night."

"And you're accusing me of murder on that—my telephone number in another man's handwriting?"

"On your own handwriting, too. When you signed M. Parker Coleman's name on the identification slip at the bank. Any expert can prove similarities."

"Why? Why would I do all this?"

"So your wife could inherit. You wanted to get your hands on the Coleman money through her."

He confronted his wife. "You don't believe a word of this, do you, Vickie?"

She could not look at him. Her eyes were squeezed shut as if in pain. He turned desperately toward Barbara and saw the look of revulsion in her face.

"What's the matter with you people?" His voice rose on a hysterical note. "What if I did get into the safe-deposit box? I did it for the family, for all of you, so you could inherit what was rightfully yours. That doesn't mean I killed Duncan or tried to frame Adam."

"You did both," I said. "I should have known after Cassidy was killed. A simple process of elimina-

tion would have told me. Lorraine wouldn't do it.
She wanted the will probated. She needed Cassidy's
testimony. And Strobe was being followed every
minute of the day by Nola's men. That's why he used
a confederate to check on me. Barbara wouldn't do
it. Nor Victoria. They would never frame their own
brother.

"Who else was left? Who would profit? You,
Dodd. Only you. Wait till the cops take your office
apart. They know how to search and they'll find the
gun and they'll prove it killed Cassidy."

His lower lip was loose and his throat muscles
working.

"And if it's more proof you want," I said, "take a
look at this. I found it in your pocket when I hung my
coat in the closet. A tire cap. Taken from the left rear
wheel of Adam's car, when you let the air out of his
tire." I sneered derisively. "After all your plans.
How could you be so stupid, so careless?"

Sudden blood congested his face. He cried out
hoarsely, "That's a lie! A damned lie! You couldn't
have found it. I threw that cap away. I. . . ."

He gasped in utter consternation, eyeballs rigid.
The collapse, when it came, was total. Fear eroded
his face, started it disintegrating.

"Oh, my God!" he said in a bankrupt whisper.
"Oh, my God!" And he bent over and covered his
face with both hands.

29

BARBARA CAME WITH ME on that fine, crisp afternoon when I visited Ruth Duncan with a check for two hundred thousand dollars. I had permission from Irving Birnbaum to make the presentation in person. He didn't mind, especially since Adam was paying his fee and not even taking his agency ten percent. Ruth Duncan cried a little and then smiled and thanked me with simple dignity.

She was curious about Dan Varney.

"My man found him in Acapulco," I told her. "He was in a panic at the thought of a jail sentence and he paid over the money, all he had left, shy some two thousand dollars, which my client gladly supplied."

"I'm putting it away for the children," she said. "That's what Fred wanted."

"Peter would make a great cop. Only three and a half years old and he broke the case."

She smiled happily. "He has a new hero now. He wants to be a lawyer."

Later, walking along with Barbara, I asked about Vickie. "How is she bearing up?"

"As well as can be expected. If Gil hadn't done that terrible thing to Adam, she would have stood beside him. She's leaving for Europe next week. She doesn't want to be here when...you know...."

When they shipped him over permanently, she meant.

"Besides, the change will help."

"It's helping Kate Wallace," I said. "She left Dan, you know, and took a job with a new agency on the coast. Doing fine, too, I hear."

"How about those two policemen?"

"Strobe and Suchak?"

"Yes."

"They resigned from the force under pressure a couple of months before they became eligible for pensions. Not enough punishment perhaps, but it hits them where they live—in the pocket."

"I wish we could have hit Lorraine there, too."

"Now, Barbara, don't be greedy. She deserves something. After all, she dropped her complaint against me to the Bar Association."

"Oh, sure, when the case collapsed."

"True. And I admit there was no possible way she could have probated your father's will. But she might have tied the estate up in litigation for a long time. You were wise in accepting a little less and making a settlement."

"We took your advice, darling."

"Will you take it again, now?"

"If it's good advice."

"The best. There are too many people in the street. Let's go home."

No argument. She linked her arm in mine and quickened her pace.

Move to Raven House...

...Home
of the Finest
in Mystery Reading!

Millions of fans can't be wrong...

For more than a century and a half,
tales of mystery and detection
have captured the imaginations
of readers the world over.

Now Raven House® Mysteries

...offers the finest examples
of this entertaining popular fiction—
in a brand-new series that contains
everything from puzzling whodunits
to stories of chilling suspense!

Reviewers across the country rave about Raven House!

"...impressive writing..."
—*Ellery Queen Magazine*

"...a joy to suspense buffs."
—*West Coast Review of Books*

"...fiendishly clever..."
—*Quality*

"...well worth the [price]..."
—*Jessyca Russell Gaver's Newsletter*

"...the best news in years for the paperback mystery field."
—*Wilson Library Bulletin*